ERWIN MORTIER (born 1965) made his mark in 1999 with his debut novel *Marcel*, which was awarded several prizes in Belgium and the Netherlands, and received acclaim throughout Europe. In the following years he quickly built up a reputation as one of the leading authors of his generation. His novel *While the Gods Were Sleeping* received the AKO Literature Prize, one of the most prestigious awards in the Netherlands. His latest work, *Stammered Songbook*, a raw yet tender elegy about illness and loss, was met with unanimous praise. Mortier's evocative descriptions bring past worlds brilliantly to life.

ERWIN MORTIER

MARCEL

Translated from the Dutch by
Ina Rilke

PUSHKIN PRESS
LONDON

Pushkin Press
71–75 Shelton Street, London WC2H 9JQ

Marcel first published in Dutch as *Marcel* by Uitgeverij
J. M. Meulenhoff bv, Amsterdam in 1999

This translation first published in 2001 by Harvill Secker
First published by Pushkin Press in 2014

0 0 1

ISBN 978 1 782270 18 8

Offset by Tetragon, London

Printed and bound by
CPI Group (UK) Ltd., Croydon CRO 4YY

www.pushkinpress.com

MARCEL

CHAPTER I

THE HOUSE LOOKED LIKE ALL THE OTHERS ON THE ROAD: sagging slightly after two centuries of habitation, driving winds and war. Behind the hedge a spine of roof tiles slumped between two gables. The windows sat a little tipsily in the walls; wooden clogs potted with petunias hung by the door.

Most of the rooms harboured a limbo of darkness, cool in summer, chilly in winter. In some, the walls had absorbed the smell of generations of cooked dinners, as in the kitchen, where grease clung to the rafters. The cellar stored, the attic forgot.

By the end of August the cold began to rise from the floors. At night there was a smell of frost in the air. Sometimes, before a downpour, the clouds skimmed so low over the roof that they seemed to be torn asunder by the finial. The light grew thin. The grass in the orchard sparkled until well after midday. The garden shrugged off its last lingering touches of colour and assumed the same grey shade as the gravestones in the churchyard nearby.

I was taken there once a year by the grandmother, but she herself was a daily visitor. It was less than five turnings between the garden gate and the place where her dead lay sleeping. She did not hold with buying flowers for All Souls' Day. There were always daisies pushing up from the graves. They would do well enough, she thought. Tombstone plaques decorated with porcelain roses filled her with scorn. She had epitaphs of her own carved in the granite of her soul.

She was the unbending midwife of her tribe. She would not allow her dead to vanish unattended. Once they were buried their bodies became earth. She raked partings in their hair and clipped the bushes by their headstones as if they were fingernails. Wedding rings had been transferred from the cold fingers of the dead to those of the warm-blooded living. She had folded their spectacles and laid them in a drawer, where they joined the tangle of all the other pairs with their long, grasshopper legs.

After each funeral she would open the curtains in the back room, raise the roller blind and put fresh sheets on the bed.

"The time will come for each and every one of us," she would say, turning back the covers. "Into bed with you, no dawdling now."

The chapel of rest had become a guest room again.

The alarm clock on the bedside table ground the seconds away. The fluorescent green face glowed spectrally in the dark. I hardly dared move between the sheets for fear of rousing the lost souls in the bedsprings, which jangled accusingly at the slightest movement of my limbs.

*

The house was a temporary annexe to heaven, due to a shortage of space. Within the confines of the glass-fronted cabinet the dead faded less rapidly than the living, whose austerely framed portraits hung unprotected on the walls of the parlour. They were not swathed in garlands of gilt or ribbons of silver, nor were they as conscientiously cherished.

All Souls' Day came four times a month at the grandmother's house. First she whisked her duster over the statue of the Virgin Mary and the miniature Yser Tower commemorating the Flemish soldiers killed in the Great War. Then she instructed me to hand her the photographs – one by one, not randomly, but in the order in which they had left their realm. They piled up. A young generation had arisen, the old one was gently falling away. In the end there were more photographs than I could hold. I laid them on the table, in the proper sequence, and patiently slid them over one at a time to be put back in the cabinet. In their ornate frames they looked like fragile carriages lining up to go through customs.

The grandmother blessed them with her duster and told me all their names. Clutches of aunts, nephews, distant cousins, nieces came up for review. Most of them were unknown to me, aside from a picture and a terminal disease. Four times a month I would listen to her reel off the same causes of death, pausing now and then to give a little sniff of resignation.

*

Bertrand was one of the few I had actually met. My first dead body. Someone had to be the first, and I could have done worse. One sunny Friday afternoon I came upon him quite rigid, hunched over the table in the low-ceilinged back kitchen of his tumbledown home. His hand was reaching for his inhaler.

"Asthma," the grandmother declared. "His lungs wheezed so loud you could hear it out in the street."

His daughter could barely wait to flog his antiques, tear the old house down and build a villa with a swimming pool.

The grandmother took a dim view of this.

"She never even lifted a finger for him." A hint of malice entered her voice, for the daughter's gleeful anticipation of her riches had been short-lived.

"Popped her clogs before the week was out. A burst appendix, it seems, after eating a boiled egg with a piece of eggshell on it. She was bent double with pain. Too mean to call a doctor, though."

Bertrand's daughter was relegated to the darkest corner of the shelf. No one was given any old place in the cramped afterlife of the cabinet, which was shared with the wine glasses and a coffee service. There was hell, paradise and purgatory. Aside from a few blessed souls who had special claims to proximity to the Virgin, no one could count on a fixed ranking. Posthumous promotion could happen, but being taken down a peg or two was more likely.

One day Bertrand too found himself in purgatory: second row, behind the Virgin's back. News had reached the grandmother of some sin he had committed.

"It seems he beat his wife."

When I asked her why, she went quiet.

"Indeed lad," she sighed at last, "why would anyone do such a thing?"

She was given to remarks like that.

"Well my dear Maurice, they won't be back, that's for sure," she would sigh.

Maurice ran a draper's shop in town, which she visited every few weeks. She always phoned first, saying: "Maurice, I need some *marchandise*. I'm coming to see you."

He would be waiting in the doorway for her to arrive. A short man, bald but for a few tufts around the ears, with a lumpy red nose over a pencil moustache. The shop window bore the name "Beernaerts Textiles" elegantly scripted in white paint.

"Getting himself worked up for one of his Italian welcomes, no doubt," the grandmother would hiss between her teeth as we rounded the corner.

She was seldom mistaken. As soon as he spotted us Maurice rushed forward, flapping his arms and rubbing his hands together. He seized the grandmother's shoulders and kissed her loudly three times.

"Whenever Andrea calls," he rejoiced, "it makes my day."

"That will do, Maurice." She glanced round to make sure there weren't too many people watching. "I'm not the Queen you know."

*

The air in the shop smelled dry. Rolls of cloth were suspended row upon row from tall racks. The floor was strewn with multicoloured pieces of thread, and the strip-lights humming on the ceiling cast a cold white glow over the fabrics.

"Come now, fellows," Maurice cried, "this floor needs sweeping. It's a right mess."

At this, several pallid assistants in grey dust-coats emerged from behind the racks, pushing wide mops that trailed beards of fluff across the floor without a sound. Sometimes I noticed them huddling together behind the racks. I could hear them sniggering at "Mijnheer" Maurice's affectations. They wore soft slippers. They padded about the shop like cats on velvet paws.

*

"I have received a bolt of serge," Maurice crowed, "Andrea my dear, it is good enough to eat. Such quality!" His fingers fluttered, fan-like, around his ears.

"It's not quite what I had in mind. I'm looking for something different. What else have you got?"

Maurice snapped his fingers. Behind the racks the assistants separated and reappeared from all sides with mildly perturbed expressions on their pale faces, as if they had been hard at work. The manager's hands flew this way and that. The assistants unhooked the shafts from the sides of the racks and released the catches. A plaintive creaking filled the air as lengths of fabric cascaded down, creating tapestried walls. The shop became a maze panelled with tweed, raw silk and velour.

Maurice escorted the grandmother down one passage and up the next, indicating the different materials with a long pointer as if they were maps of strange continents. Every few steps he motioned to his assistants to continue the display, whereupon they swung their shafts and released yet more walls of fabric. Whenever the grandmother slowed her pace he snatched up the material in both hands and held it under her nose.

She rubbed it between thumb and forefinger, sniffed it, and came very close to taking a bite.

"Samples?" she said.

He reached under the rack for the book of swatches. Turning the pages he escorted the grandmother across his emporium back to the window, where they inspected each sample in turn.

"Daylight cannot tell a lie," the grandmother said.

They moved closer together. Maurice's head swung from left to right in time with his hands.

The grandmother muttered something.

Maurice shrugged and raised his eyebrows.

The grandmother shook her head, giving her hat a stern little shake in the process.

"*Bon*, I've made up my mind," she said finally.

They crossed side by side to the long wooden counter. Maurice noted down her order on a sheet of brown paper. Each item filled him with delight.

"And I need some more of those *perlefine* beads," the grandmother said. "I've run out again."

He grinned.

"You know what they're like in the country," she said brightly. "Anything gaudy and glittery makes them feel rich."

Maurice manoeuvred a stepladder between the counter and the wall fitment made up of countless little drawers.

"Yes," he said, "there's not much demand for such items around here. I always keep the country things somewhere at the top."

They exchanged grins.

"*Perlefines, perlefines.*" He opened a drawer. "How many do you need?"

"A good supply."

He filled a paper bag with the tear-shaped beads strung on glistening thread and cautiously descended the ladder.

"*Voila*! Finery for country lasses. Can I offer you a glass of something?"

*

A long windowless passage led to a dimly lit sitting room, where Maurice poured himself a snifter of cognac. The grandmother opted for Elixir, a colourless liquid that clung to the sides of the small glass.

"Well now," she said, her cheeks flushing a deep pink, "that goes down a treat, I must say."

They sat facing each other at a long table by the window. Small flowerpots with Mother-in-law's Tongues were lined up on the sill.

I was not listening to their conversation. I had been given a glass of grass-green lemonade and a magazine with pictures of Monte Carlo to keep me occupied.

"When?" I heard Maurice moan. "When, when, when?"

With each "when" he banged his fists on the table. "The answer is: never. The licence is still in my brother's name, dammit!"

"There, there Maurice, no need to get all excited."

"I've paid my dues, haven't I?"

He stared out of the window. It was drizzling. Women in nylon raincoats moved past the sansevierias. He topped up their glasses.

"Not so full, not so full," the grandmother cried. "It goes down far too easily."

The rain drew slanting stripes across the window. The stripes merged. People opened their umbrellas. Others, ghost-like, hurried by holding shopping bags over their heads.

Maurice and the grandmother talked in whispers. Their voices blended with the pattering rain, rising now and then.

"They're the ones who took advantage," the grandmother sniffed. "You can guess who's taken to driving a Mercedes, can't you Maurice? A Mercedes, no less."

A brief silence ensued.

Then Maurice said something odd.

It sounded like: "Hee."

Silence.

Again he said: "Hee."

When I dared raise my head I caught a glimpse of him stuffing his handkerchief into the pocket of his dust-coat. He threw the grandmother a red-eyed, helpless look, uncorked the bottle and poured himself another drink.

The grandmother declined a refill, covering her glass with her hand. Maurice emptied his cognac in one draught and sank into silence. He inhaled through gritted teeth. A last stifled sob sent a shudder through his body.

The grandmother stood up, adjusted her hat and shook the creases out of her skirt.

"Indeed, Maurice, indeed," she said at last. "There's no turning the clock back, is there?"

"He still hasn't got over it," she declared to no one in

particular as we walked back to the railway station. "Whatever would Agnes say?"

*

Agnes wore black satin; she had a white face and large eyes behind thick glasses. She smiled wanly from the display cabinet, baring brown teeth. Her son Léon, in his early twenties, stared out at the world from the shop front, where he stood arm in arm with Marcel, the grandmother's youngest brother. They were pals, their destinies as yet undecided. They shared the same shiny black frame, at the foot of the Yser Tower.

"The war had already begun by then," the grandmother remarked. "Léon was an only child. Maurice certainly had his share of misfortune, poor soul."

They had wanted another son. Agnes was nearly forty at the time. Too old really, the grandmother thought, but what can you expect, she couldn't get over her boy's death. Things didn't turn out well.

"It was like a donkey's pregnancy. Thirteen, fourteen months and no contractions. Agnes said: 'It'll come in its own good time.' She carried on for a year and a half, poor thing. In the end they cut her open, but it had gone rock-hard."

They cut her open, but it had gone rock-hard. I imagined doctors and nurses letting fly with hammers and chisels in an attempt to excavate a stone foetus from Agnes' fleshy insides. I did not dare ask if they had installed it on Agnes' tombstone. It would not have surprised me if they had.

*

"Turned to rock indeed," chuckled Stella, a cousin several

times removed and the maid of all work. On Saturdays she swung the chairs up on the table and herded the settees into a corner, on top of which she draped the carpet. From the cupboard under the stairs she extracted floor cloths and mops and scouring brushes with ginger, military moustaches. She doused the black tiles with buckets of white suds, and set about scrubbing hard.

"Don't you go ruining my tiles now, Stella," the grandmother admonished her.

They were like a comic double act. The grandmother, tall and angular and overbearing, with an air of worldly superiority over her distant relative, and Stella, a short, sharp-edged blade of grass. To make herself taller she fashioned a bun with a hairpiece and wadding on top of her head. Most of the time she wore owlish spectacles on her nose, giving her a cross look that belied her nature.

*

"Turned to rock indeed!"

It was morning. Her spectacles lay idle on the dressing table among her boxes of face powder. In a corner of the room a bare-headed, shadowy figure sat on a creaking sofa, shaking uncontrollably: her husband Lucien. He would wear out three more sofas after that – one every six months, until the springs fell out of the bottom and his heart gave up for good.

He was afflicted with a strange disease that later on, once his portrait had joined the queue for dusting, would give the grandmother cause to vent her morbid pride. She would remark that he was "related by marriage, of course." That made a difference, apparently.

"There's nothing we can do for him," the neurologist told Stella. "Your husband suffers from Huntington's Chorea."

"How do you mean, Korea?" Stella's tears and bafflement lasted for months. "How can that be? My Lucien never, ever went to Korea."

*

"The little one just shrivelled up, understand?" Stella said. "Come along now, why don't you give me a hand. Here, hold this."

She fixed the hairnet over the false bun, bowed her head, reached for my hands and pressed my fingers down around the net, which she proceeded to secure with hairpins plucked from the corner of her mouth. She had arranged all the false curls around the wadding and pulled her own hair up tight to form a sort of pinnacle on top.

I longed to touch her head with the palm of my hand, especially in the early morning when her hair would be hanging loose, still smelling of the night.

In the mirror I glimpsed tufts of underarm hair protruding from the short sleeves of her green summer frock, and caught a pungent whiff of armpits.

She knitted her brow and clamped her lips tightly on the hairpins. On her knees, with both hands on her head, she might have been a supplicant, or a prisoner held at gunpoint.

*

Stella contributed her own epitaphs to the grandmother's weekly valedictions.

"Poor lambs, it's been such a long time . . . " she would sigh as the duster slid over a delicate gilt frame of acanthus leaves, out of which three angelic boys gazed earnestly into space.

"Our Noel, our Antoine and our Valère. My brothers," the grandmother said.

I could see the resemblance in her jutting cheekbones, her strong chin. Their eyes in a haze of curly blonde hair glowed with an unnatural brightness.

"If they'd known about penicillin in those days," Stella said, "they'd still be with us, poor things. The croup, ooh it was dreadful. Lucien had it too. The doctor told his mother to hold him upside down over a tub of boiling water. Did he scream!"

"Boiling water with a few drops of eucalyptus, oh yes, my mother used to do that too. Still . . . My father buried them at the bottom of the garden. All three of them, side by side under a white gravestone. By the beech tree. That was still allowed in those days."

She would have turned her garden into a graveyard given the chance, so that she might sail from grave to grave among the rose-beds, day in day out, armed with scouring powder and bleach to kill the moss. Flanking the picture of the three boys were the grandmother's father and mother – railway accident and cancer of the bone – one under each of the Virgin's hands. The grandmother's mother wore her hair swept into a bun on the top of her head. Her father wore a shiny pin on his necktie.

*

Sometimes, when Stella took my place handing over the pictures one by one, I would crawl under the table and lie back on the bare tiled floor, breathing the fresh smell of a just-cleaned house. When boredom crept over me the floor would reveal its secret geography, complete with all the tiny ridges and ravines where the soapy water collected into miniature lakes. It was then that I discovered that every movement in the house followed a fixed pattern. Everyone traced habitual paths, skirts billowing round calves, shoes creaking with every step. I would lie there flat on my back until my muscles became rigid with cold and the space between the table legs turned into an Egyptian tomb, monumental and forbidding.

*

"Our Cécile, she's so earnest-looking," Stella said.

Cécile, Sister Marie-Cécile, was the only living person to be granted admission to the display cabinet. She wore a crown of white lilies. It was the day of her investiture as a nun. She struck a solemn pose in the convent garden, a sickly Bride of Jesus, about to be entered in the dry annals of eternity.

"A stick with a wimple," my father grumbled sometimes. He was not much taken with her.

"Our Cécile inhabits saintly spheres," the grandmother said, feigning reverence.

Once a year Sister Cécile received a visit from her family. The grandmother loaded the boot of my father's Ford Anglia with jars of preserves. My mother buckled her safety belt with undisguised reluctance and whispered: "Right, let's be off."

The convent was a sprawling brick building on a hill. The car chugged noisily up the incline. A pull on the bell handle sent a tinkling ring down long corridors. It was several minutes before the heavy wooden door was opened by a nun bent double with age.

There was a long walled garden with cedars and benches in the shade, occupied by a number of old biddies chewing their lips. Now and then one of them got up and did a little waltz on the flagstones, while her sisters moved their swaddled legs in three-quarter time.

Sister Cécile's quarters were at the top of the building, right under the eaves. Tortuous flights and a succession of ever narrower corridors took us upstairs, past crowded dormitories smelling of urine. At the end of the last corridor a few steps led up to a door. The nun had heard us coming, for she came out to greet her visitors.

"Ah, there you are."

She placed her hands devoutly on her chest. A stick with a wimple, mummified already. A sallow face, drained of expression by a life of every conceivable abstention.

"Come in, come in," she murmured.

She had toned her voice down to a permanent whisper, mouse-grey mutterings from an anaemic rodent of the Lord.

Her narrow room was furnished with hard cane chairs. On a table stood a thermos containing watery coffee. Little hisses escaped from the lid. In the heat the tiles on the roof made a ticking sound behind the insulation panels.

The nun poured coffee. She plied me with Sacred Heart memorial cards, stale ginger biscuits and mildewed chocolates. She took a biscuit herself, which she dipped in her coffee, and I had a strong sensation in my own mouth of her tongue flattening the sugary mush against her palate.

The nun chuckled and then announced gravely: "I can't open my mouth very wide. I've just had an operation on my jaw."

My father rolled his eyes. I could see him thinking: she'll have us operated on for our faith next, the witch, but he saved his remark for later, in the car.

"If only she'll spare us her communion with the Holy Ghost," he had said on the way there. "And I hope to God she shuts up about her miracles."

Once a month it was Sister Cécile's turn to help the elderly nuns in bath chairs into the chapel. She invoked the Holy Ghost so ecstatically that one of the old girls slid from her seat and crumpled into a dribbling heap on the floor.

"Speaking in tongues. Saw it with my own eyes." For once her voice shot up. "Glossolalia!"

Epilepsy, according to the local GP.

The nun had her own way of honouring the dead. She saw herself as the family prayer-wheel. From her hilltop she sent a never-ending stream of invocations to heaven. Her façade of humility displayed small cracks now and then, from which oozed unspoken reproof.

"That boy," she said, "has been lying there all alone for so many years now. I remember him in my prayers every day. He saved us from Bolshevism."

I thought she was referring to yet another mysterious disease.

*

In the display cabinet at home Cécile posed next to Brother Armand, who was wearing his black Benedictine habit for the occasion. When attending funerals he usually wore it over his civilian clothes, and more often than not he would raise a laugh.

"Someone ought to tell him to take off his bicycle clips," the grandmother remarked with a sigh each time he swanned up to the altar for an oblation, flashing white calves and ankles.

He never missed a mass for the dead. No one could snivel the way he did. It was a brief homage, no more. After the service there would be the meal with the mourners, and the wine. One day it was his turn to be mourned. The bells in the abbey tower tolled a sonorous knell. "He brought a spirit of generosity to our monastery," intoned the abbot, visibly relieved to be rid of the smell of alcohol.

*

When all the pictures had been properly dusted the grandmother closed the glass wings of her cabinet. She had reflected, reassessed and rearranged. She had piled proof upon proof, for and against Death, who was both her enemy and her most loyal ally. Death robbed her of her relatives, but he also fixed them in still poses ensuring that they would meekly undergo her domestic ministrations.

When I saw my face reflected in the glass it was a fleeting glimpse, with far less substance than the images of the dear departed. Especially when, every few months, Stella and the grandmother, in a fit of nostalgia, ransacked drawers and cupboards for still more photographs. In no time the table would be thickly carpeted with pictures in which the past jostled indiscriminately with the present. One showed a coffin emerging from the green front door. In another, boys wearing clogs and girls with ribbons in their hair frolicked on the same doorstep. Here the season's first asparagus was being harvested, there a trench in the war-torn orchard was being filled by a shadowy figure with a shovel.

The house, having detached itself from the world at large, became the repository of all those albums. In the midst of all the snapshots, I could easily imagine slipping out of that dark front door, down the well-worn path in the grass, past the blood-red garden fence into the orchard, where apples dropped like hand grenades from the branches, the same branches that were draped in blossomy parachutes in spring.

My own likeness cropped up regularly in that profusion of images. Me being lifted out of a baby bath by my mother. My mother holding my arms while I try to walk unsteadily across the floor – stark-naked, not yet a year old, three decades younger than the faded yellow curtains on the window overlooking the back yard. I began to read an obfuscated sadness into the palm-frond wallpaper, stained with time. Our first fridge must be humming somewhere out of the picture.

Those snapshots would have been taken by my father. Perhaps he had leaned back against the marble sill just visible under the dusty net curtains, waiting for me to look up at him and smile.

The flash used to startle me, Stella said, just as it had startled my great-grandparents. They lay at opposite ends of the table, their eyes not lowered like my mother's, for they stared fixedly into the lens with unconcealed suspicion.

They wore their Sunday best for their respective portraits

taken when they were aged about eighteen. They did so again on the day of their engagement, when they posed together for a studio photograph against a backdrop of cardboard columns and leafy boughs. Their peasant pride sat uncomfortably with the Arcadian setting – hazier now, after a century, and dull in places.

Sixty years later and on their last legs they face the camera again, as stiffly as ever, to bear witness to their eldest great-grandchild's first steps. Just as vulnerable, just as bereft of the underpinnings of language, they strain to assume an appropriate expression, strike the right attitude, put on the proper airs. Their dignified stance reminds me of starched bedlinen and locked wardrobes.

At some point in their lives, between the Arcadian props and the crutches, my great-grandparents pose for a picture on either side of Marcel. He is about sixteen years old, an acne-ridden teenager in plus fours. One raised hand shades his eyes from the sun, which has half obliterated him already.

CHAPTER 2

ON FRIDAYS AFTER SCHOOL I USUALLY HUNG AROUND in the attic or skulked in one of the rooms, bored stiff. Until the peal of Miss Veegaete's laughter made me jump to my feet. Twice a year she ordered a new frock from the grandmother.

The blinds were half lowered. On Fridays the grandmother's abode was transformed into a dimly lit palace, a dusky, formal venue for mysterious conclaves.

It was usually Stella who answered the door. She would be wearing one of her tight, unflattering blouses so as to "look nice for the clientele", as well as sparkly earrings and high-heeled shoes. Her heels would beat a nervous tattoo from the front door down the echoing passage, taking in the kitchen on her way to the sewing room where the grandmother held court. She became a girl again, dressing up in her mother's clothes, putting too much rouge on her cheeks. On Fridays she made her topknot even taller, like an Indian temple, but the effect was spoilt by her stern round spectacles.

The grandmother was ready to receive her callers. She had made a display of fashion magazines, pattern books and squares of soft fabric on the table by the big window facing north, for daylight cannot tell a lie. It made no difference whether it was summer or winter. Miss Veegaete ordered her light dress in the dead of winter, and it would be midsummer when she called to discuss her autumn requirements.

The arcane manipulations that took place in the sewing room were not intended for Miss Veegaete's eyes. She was shielded from the sight of the wasps' nest of pins, the snakepit of limp zip fasteners in the drawer, the little boxes overflowing with enamel and mother-of-pearl buttons on the high shelves. At the end of each working day the snippets of dress material and tangled threads lying in frivolous anarchy on the floor were swept into a heap for the rag-and-bone man. Clients were admitted to the sewing room only to have their measurements taken. They would be offered magazines to leaf through, which then gave them the illusion of knowing what they wanted. But it was the grandmother who knew what they wanted. She dazzled her ladies with the sheer variety and glamour of the designs. She reeled off the names of fabrics like prayers, muttering things about the potential for pleats or the merits of cutting on the bias until the client got confused and asked: "Would that suit me, do you think?"

"We'll see what we can do. Stella my dear, why don't you brew us a good pot of coffee. And we'd like some cake, too. *Madame* and I have things to discuss."

Each Friday, in a ceremony that was repeated three or four times, the expensive gold-rimmed coffee service would progress from the glass cabinet to the large tray shivering in Stella's skinny hands, from the tray to the coffee table, and from the coffee table to the kitchen where the cups were washed before returning to the cabinet. The removal of all the stage-props, followed by their reappearance for the benefit of a fresh audience, took place every hour or so. Each visitor in turn was made a fuss of. Stella's occasional disparaging remarks would earn her a lecture.

"As far as I am concerned," the grandmother said, "every single client, even the simplest farmer's wife, is a duchess, a baroness in her own right. They all want something special. Imagine the scene if they met here by accident! They'd be bound to think I was copying the same garment, not creating custom-made fashion."

"I'll go and wash the dishes," Stella said gruffly. As the afternoon wore on she kept fiddling with her earrings. "They don't half itch when you get sweaty."

*

The serving of coffee was supposed to soften the embattled client until she was putty in the hands of her hostesses. The grandmother pretended to think long and hard, although she knew exactly which bolts from Maurice's shop she kept stored in her attic.

"I've got an idea," she would say in her stage voice. "I've just thought of something that would be most suitable for that design I showed you a moment ago. Not too expensive, good quality, and quite distinctive."

If, after coffee, the client was still dithering, Stella could be relied upon to get things moving. She would say something outrageous while measurements were being taken in front of the mirror. She and the grandmother made an excellent team. They homed in on the client, biding their time like cats with tails of fluttering measuring tape.

"Shouldn't the skirt be just a little shorter?" the client asked.

"I'd leave the hem a bit lower, if I were you," said the grandmother, glancing knowingly over the woman's shoulders in the mirror.

"Oh. But I was thinking of something a bit shorter, just for a change."

"Well," sighed the grandmother, "of course it's entirely up to you. If you're sure. However, the problem is, if you want a short skirt, it'll have to be really short."

The client, retreating into silence, studied her reflection.

"Knee-length wouldn't suit you," Stella said, taking her cue from the grandmother. "Your knees are too plump."

"Too plump," echoed the grandmother, "not really, I wouldn't call them plump. It's the fabric, *Madame*. Look."

She draped the material around the woman's hips.

"If it's a short skirt you want, and you still want pleats, it won't look very smart." She crumpled a handful of fabric in her fist.

"See what I mean? I can of course make a few tucks here and there, but still – I'm afraid it'll look like some sort of school uniform. Now let's see, if we drop the hem a bit – look! – it'll all turn out a treat. A short skirt of this material, *Madame*, would be a dreadful waste. And you must admit the quality is excellent. It would be a shame not to use it to its best advantage."

"I suppose you're right . . ." the client faltered, struggling to reconcile the picture in her head with her plump knees.

Stella held her tongue. So did the grandmother. Cowed into

submission, the client was ready for the *coup de grâce*, which was painless, for it was expertly wrapped in layers of velvet.

"It'll turn out wonderfully," the grandmother promised, "I can feel it in my bones."

*

Late in the evening, when peace was restored, they would let their hair down.

"God forbid that I should give in to everything they wanted, whatever would they look like! Frights! A guardian of good taste, that's what I am. I can't go ruining my reputation, can I?"

One day I had the temerity to ask, in the presence of a client, whether the material with splashy flowers was going to be used for kitchen curtains. She had boxed my ears on previous occasions, but this time it hurt.

Mondays were devoted to pattern drawing, design adjustments and the strategic deployment of pins so as to hide unwanted prominences.

"A good garment," she affirmed with deeply held conviction, "both conceals and reveals."

There was no one to hear her secret formulas, her mutterings and hummed tunes as she breathed life into one garment after another. The sewing room was transformed into a magical laboratory, and she into an alchemist. She drew lines with a stick of greasy chalk on feather-light sheets of tissue paper laid out on the table. She guided the predatory jaws of her scissors around the contours of a skirt or the lily-like outline of a bridal gown.

"Sheffield Steel," she purred. "Sheffield Steel is the very best."

Stella was charged with basting the cut segments. The grandmother spread a fresh length of material on the table and set about plotting new graphs.

*

Miss Veegaete was unlike the other clients. Miss Veegaete, the grandmother said, was what you might call a *bijou* of a client.

"It's always plain sailing with her. You can tell right off she's a lady. She's got city manners."

"She taught at a school in Brussels once," Stella said. "A posh boarding school run by Insuline Nuns."

"Ursuline, Stella. Ursuline."

"Whatever. A school for rich folk. They spoke French! D'you know how they say Miss Veegaete in French? Haven't you heard? They pronounce it *Veekàt.* They call her *Mademoiselle Veekàt.* She's got a piano at home, did you know?"

Miss Veegaete was well aware of her status as honoured visitor and privileged client. When she rang the bell the door flew open at once. Stella, tottering on stiletto heels, would help her out of her coat.

"Do step into the salon," she would say, "Andrea will be right with you."

Anything Miss Veegaete said was lapped up by the grandmother as if it were liquid gold.

"How right you are," was her unvarying reply.

Cake was served, with cherry filling and a generous dollop of whipped cream. The fragile porcelain coffee cups seemed to gain in translucence whenever Miss Veegaete raised hers to her lips. She was a giant honey bird, large and feathered, a hummingbird-turned-woman. As she tasted the cake a high-pitched sound rose up from the underhang of her chin. "Divine," she churred. "Heavenly."

*

On such days, when the door was ajar, I would slip into the room like a shadow. I lingered in the half-light to prolong the sensation of being unseen and all-seeing. By the sheer concentration of my gaze, I imagined, I could make Miss Veegaete turn round on the sofa padded with embroidered cushions to face me and say: "*Mais voilà. Notre petit prince. Quel surprise, mon ami.*"

"Go and shake hands now," the grandmother instructed.

"Good afternoon Miss Veegaete."

"*Bonjour, mon élève.*"

Her hands fluttered briefly around my chin towards my cheeks, as if she were about to lift me up by my ears. For an instant I saw her pout her lips and make to lean forward, but she changed her mind.

"Is he tongue-tied in class too?" the grandmother asked wryly.

"Not really. He can be quite a chatterbox at times, can't he?" Her fingers hovered over the top of my head. "But we can't complain."

"Have a piece of cake, dear," the grandmother said. "Off you go and eat it in the kitchen, because I know what you're like. Always spilling things. And mind you wash your hands first. Look at you, your paws are filthy – you're in no state to shake hands with a lady!"

"Been rummaging in the attic, I shouldn't wonder," said Stella. "Odd isn't it? The way he holes up in the attic all the time."

"Ah well, he's a dreamer, isn't he," Miss Veegaete said with a wink. "Daydreaming – that's something he and I have in common."

Her laugh dropped like a lark from the sky and her shoes gave a little creak as she curled up her toes. She had chubby feet. In the summer she wore sturdy sandals, the kind worn by children. The strap pressed into her plump ankles and her toes lay like a row of bosoms in a black leather corset.

Nothing could be whiter than Miss Veegaete's thighs, of which I caught an occasional fleeting glimpse in the classroom, from my seat in the front row right under her desk on the blue stone platform. The whiteness veered between milky clouds and marble with pale meandering veins.

On hot afternoons when the awnings were out over the windows, Miss Veegaete would sink onto her chair with a sigh as she abandoned herself to digesting her lunch. She lived in a house overlooking the playground. At midday I would see her sitting with her brother and elder sister Louise at the table by the dining room window, eating soup and munching thick slices of bread. No wonder Miss Veegaete dozed off in the afternoon. She would prop up her chin with her hands and let her eyelids droop. Now and then an ominous glug-glug would escape her, as if in the depths of her stomach, under the flowery skirt, a thick porridge was dripping slowly from one grotto to the next. Miss Veegaete pretended not to notice. She was ladylike.

On other afternoons Miss Veegaete would read, giving little sighs of contentment, as if she were blowing bubbles. When she was completely engrossed in her book she would unthinkingly pass her tongue over her teeth to dislodge bits of bread, making her cheeks bulge in all directions as if she were sucking a large boiled sweet.

It was when she was reading that I had the best chance of getting a look-in. Only then her thighs might part ever so slightly, making her skirt pull taut across her knees. From there her thighs receded into darkness. At some point at the back those two massive columns were joined together. But I had to put my head all the way down with my cheek almost touching the desk to get even the smallest peek, by which time Miss Veegaete had usually glanced up from her book and smacked her knees together again.

After an hour of mounting, bleary-eyed boredom, the gurgling of her intestines subsided. Shutting the book to banish all thoughts of siesta, she drew herself up. She did so deliberately and slowly, as if her body were being inflated with some strange gas. Next minute she was tripping through the classroom on her sandals, squeezing her ample body between the desks. When she leaned forward over my shoulders the silky fabric of her blouse brushed my neck and hair. It was a thin blouse with voluptuous flowers in pastel shades and lianas snaking across her breasts. A jungle from Maurice's stockroom.

*

"Only the best is good enough for Miss Veegaete," the grandmother said.

Stella admired Miss Veegaete's full figure.

"Everything looks good on her. *Mademoiselle Veekàt*. Even her name suits her. If I had a name like that I'd ask for a raise."

"Indeed," said the grandmother with a chuckle, "but your name isn't like that. Do you know what yours sounds like in French? Pom. See how far that will get you."

"What do you mean, Pom?"

"Apple is 'pom' in French. Stella Pom. Hardly a name that'll get you a raise, eh?"

*

When Miss Veegaete had had her fill of cake it was time to get down to business. The three women put their heads together in the parlour, flapping their fashion magazines.

"I rather like wide sleeves," Miss Veegaete said. "They hide my upper arms. But I'm not so keen on them being wide around the wrists."

The grandmother spoke reassuringly.

"We can always do a large cuff, you know, with two or three buttonholes. I've got the perfect buttons for that style of blouse. And what do you have in mind for the skirt?"

More riffling of pages. The grandmother snapped her fingers for Stella to bring her the samples. The different fabrics were held up to the light in the narrow parting between the curtains, they were draped on Miss Veegaete's shoulders, held against her legs, laid across her stomach and chest. Wearing all these patches Miss Veegaete turned into a tortoiseshell cat.

"I'll leave it to you to select the material, Andrea," she said weakly.

The grandmother hid her satisfaction by plunging her hands into the pockets of her apron.

Miss Veegaete was finding it hard to make up her mind. "Tartan is lovely, but it doesn't suit me."

"I'll find you a tartan that does suit you," the grandmother said firmly. "There are tartans and tartans."

The fabrics passed through all three pairs of hands while the grandmother gave a running commentary. The pinafore she wore over her best dress clinked with the regalia of her trade: thimbles, scissors and the little clothes-brush that had velvet pile instead of bristles, with which she gave the garments a final stroke before they left the premises.

"We'll make a tuck right here," I heard her mutter. "We'll line it, too, that'll do a world of good . . ." "A well-made *plissé* is a gem . . ." "If we have a flat yoke, the front can be shirred."

Stella grew impatient.

"It's time we took your measurements. You're not planning on going on a diet or anything?"

"A diet?" Miss Veegaete giggled.

Rising from the sofa she seemed to be preparing a curtsey, with her arms describing arcs in the air.

"Lose weight? *Moi*? How can I if you keep offering me all those goodies?"

*

They moved to the sewing room, where a great many more samples were met with twitters of approval.

"Ah, cashmere. If I had the money I'd wear cashmere all the time."

"You want to watch out with cashmere," the grandmother said. "A lot of inferior stuff goes by that name nowadays. So-called cashmere."

Miss Veegaete peeled off her cardigan. I prayed they would

forget about me for once. I slunk to the corner between the wardrobe and the wall, sank to my knees and vanished under the sewing table.

"Do you still buy from Maurice?" Miss Veegaete asked.

She bent down, undid the buckles of her shoes and pinched her stockings out from between her toes. "And how is Maurice these days?"

"Ups and downs, you know how it is. Nothing much has changed. What do you expect?"

"Poor Maurice," Miss Veegaete said dreamily. "Such a flourishing business, and yet he still hasn't got his licence back."

She drew herself up again.

"It's . . ." she tried to think of a suitable word while she unbuttoned her sleeves,

" . . . odious, that's what it is. Odious!"

"It is indeed," Stella echoed.

"And you're rather odious too, young man."

The grandmother lifted a corner of the tablecloth and gave me an icy stare.

"Off you go and play in the garden, now. No need for menfolk here. Besides, you're far too young to care about skirts."

"Heavens above," Miss Veegaete cried. "I hadn't even noticed he was there."

I sloped off, hanging my head.

"You don't mean to say you take an interest in ladies already? At your age!"

She turned to the grandmother.

"He's very forward – and not only with his reading either, I see. The boy is a genius."

"When all is said and done," the grandmother remarked, "they're all geniuses."

"Polite boys leave the room without being told," hissed Stella, shutting the door behind me with a bang.

*

I pressed my ear against the door to hear what they were saying, without much success. The doors in the house were solid, pre-war quality, and although Stella was quite thin her back almost completely blocked my view through the keyhole. All I could hear were whispers, the rustle of Miss Veegaete shedding her clothes, the swish of her satin slip, which would be white or *vieux rose*.

"My brother was lucky," I heard her say. "He was only seventeen at the time."

"There were plenty of others they didn't let off so lightly," the grandmother retorted. "They picked on Maurice just to make themselves look better. Every single textile firm made money off the Germans. Good money, too."

"All those little men in the camps on television," Stella blurted, "where d'you suppose the material for all those striped pyjamas came from? Am I right, Andrea?"

"Whenever I see those old films," the grandmother said, "I think: there goes the Flanders rag trade. And who gets the blame? Maurice. Or me."

"They always blame the ordinary folk," Miss Veegaete chimed in. "Nothing new there. Anyway, it's not a question of blame, is it?"

I didn't catch what the grandmother said. Her voice was drowned in the clatter of buttons spilling from a box.

"Stella! What a butterfingers you are! That's the second time you've sent those buttons flying."

"I can't think straight today," Stella moaned. "It's the heat. I'm sweating my heart out."

She bent down to collect the buttons off the floor.

Miss Veegaete stood in front of the mirror, stroking her neck with both hands. Her bosom burgeoned inside her satin bodice. "Marcel was old enough to know what he was doing, Andrea. He was twenty-four. Not a youngster anymore."

"No indeed," the grandmother said tartly. "But it didn't do us Flemings any good, that's all I can say."

"We'll get there in the end," Miss Veegaete said soothingly. "Of course we will. We do our best. Which of us knows French better than Flemish, anyway?"

"Not me!" barked Stella.

"You mind your own business," hissed the grandmother.

"There's nothing to be ashamed of," Miss Veegaete went on. "I have always spoken my mind. Everywhere. Even in Brussels. Even in the classroom with my girls from good families. Fair and square, I always used to say."

She stepped into her shoes, dragging the heels over the tiled floor.

"Now then, let's measure your waist," the grandmother said.

*

There was nothing square about Miss Veegaete. She was all curves and hollows. Sometimes, when she was reading in class and thought no one was watching, she would slip off her shoes. Crossing one leg over the other and holding her book with one hand, she reached under the desk with the other and gave her ankle-strap a firm tug to undo the buckle. Without raising her eyes from her book she clapped her knees together again, placed the point of one shoe against the heel of the other, and released each foot from its prison with a soft, squelching sound.

When the postprandial torpor wore off and the fidgeting in the classroom mounted, her stockinged feet felt around for her shoes. She balanced them on her toes and gave them a little shake before slipping them on and fastening the straps. She smoothed the shoulders of her blouse and clapped her hands for attention.

"Put down your pencils, now!' she commanded.

She went round the classroom collecting sheets of paper, pausing here and there to bestow praise on a drawing: boxy houses, stiff-legged figures in gardens full of trees with huge fruits, under blazing suns with straw-coloured rays.

I hated colour, so I did every thing in black. I had made a drawing of the grandmother's house, but without the front so you could see all the rooms and what was in them. I had put Marcel into the picture, too: Marcel in the attic wearing a helmet and scary bat's wings.

"Er . . ." murmured Miss Veegaete, "it is, how shall I put it, artistic."

When she had finished pinning all the drawings to a board at the back of the classroom she swept to the door and flung it open.

She clapped her hands again: "Time to be excused!"

The boys poured from their desks towards the door, where the jostling throng assembled into a double file.

"Forward march!"

She drove her flock down the corridor, along the windowsills with potted geraniums and discarded lunch boxes, past the coat racks with mackintoshes dangling from the pegs like hooded cassocks. Talking was not allowed.

We trooped down the stairs and turned into another corridor past a classroom full of boys reciting tables in voices that were already breaking.

Halfway down the final corridor I sniffed the reek of the latrines: a sickly smell of urine masked by clouds of jasmine spray. I clenched my buttocks instinctively.

Miss Veegaete lined up her class in front of six cubicles with short doors. Adjoining them was her own private lavatory, with a door that reached down to the floor. She clapped her hands a third time, whereupon the front ranks vanished into the cubicles. Six pairs of shoes were draped first in corduroy or denim, then in underpants of all colours, after which six little streams splashed into the pans.

"And what do we do when we've finished?"

Six waterfalls cascaded in chorus.

Miss Veegaete always waited for the last pupils to take their turn in the cubicles before locking herself in the mother of all lavatories, which had a toilet higher than the others. I was fumbling with my flies in the cubicle next to hers, with only a flimsy partition between us.

I could hear Miss Veegaete hitch up her skirt, then her petticoat. She was having trouble pulling down her underwear; the material kept getting twisted in the elastic.

I heard a grunt in the cubicle on the other side, signalling a Number Two, then a heavy plop and a sigh of relief.

I waited, elbows on knees, counting the specks in the tiles at my feet. Miss Veegaete would be lowering herself onto the toilet. I pictured her thighs spreading over the seat. A hen sitting on her brood.

Elsewhere I heard belts being buckled.

It seemed an eternity before it came: a wide, motherly stream issuing from a cleft in the rocks, splashing into the pan, tinkling like her laughter.

The world stood still. The hot ache in my groin became a whirlpool, a funnel. The blood rushed to my cheeks, tears stung my eyes. My own water joined Miss Veegaete's finale in a plashing duet.

At the end I waited.

A drop of mine.

A drop of hers.

Then came the rasp of paper in the depths of her thighs, against hairs that did not bear thinking about.

CHAPTER 3

POTATOES KEPT SHOOTING UP ALL OVER THE GARDEN, year after year. They sprouted in the most unexpected places, under the trees and among the dahlias, even in the rock garden surrounding the Virgin's grotto, where the purplish shoots grew spindly, craning upwards to the light.

The grandmother hacked at them with her trowel. "Goodness knows where the brutes keep coming from."

She poked around until she found the tuber, which she trampled fiercely to a pulp. "At least that makes one less."

I wondered if there had ever been a potato age, the way there had been ice ages. An age when the land was carpeted with potato plants as far as the eye could see, all of them with tubers slumbering in the soil. Perhaps they were trying, from their base in the vegetable patch, their last stronghold, to reconquer the garden.

All year round the grandmother observed a strict segregation between two domains. The sewing room with its garments on hangers and dressmaker's dummies extended beyond the big window into the garden, where leafy crowns dipped and swayed like hooped petticoats in the wind. A tracery of paths skirting the trees led to the gate in the hedge. Further away, in the full sun, lay a straight-lined configuration of plots.

The vegetable patch was the grandfather's domain – or rather, his codicil. When they were married the grandmother grudgingly accorded him the use of the old bleaching field. He dug it all up, raised the beds, deposited barrowfuls of stable manure and planted his potatoes. He also brought his entire family with him. The Eggermonts. Desperados, loafers and adventurers they were. Interlopers in the garden of the grandfather's wife and the other members of her tough tribe, the Ornelises.

In the summer the two families gathered uneasily around the long table in the orchard. Fingers shot up in the air, fists thumped the table top. The Ornelises crossed their arms and gritted their teeth. They fretted and ground their heels in the grass. The Eggermonts stamped their feet and jiggled their knees against the underside of the table, their eyes smouldering with self-righteousness. In the background loomed the debris of shattered illusions.

The arguments were always about politics, of which I knew nothing as yet. My father took a picture with his new Kodak, but it was not until much later that I understood its portent. One side of the table under the cherry blossom is a forest of flailing arms and flushed heads. The other side is occupied by the Ornelises, holding their tongues, eyes narrowed to slits in lined, weather-beaten faces. The two camps are divided by a wavering frontier of plates and glasses running from one end of the checked tablecloth to the other. Presiding at the head is the grandmother, darkly aloof like the trees in her garden. Her genteel manners are being furtively mocked along one side of the table, while the other side bridles with reproach at her having married beneath her. Her elbows are propped on the table, her mouth is hidden behind her clasped hands.

*

The grandmother saw me as one of hers, as an Ornelis. She would set things right. She taught me to weed. I trailed after her down the garden paths. She moved with the majesty of an ancient galleon, veering from port to starboard and back again, pointing out herbs and plants in the border.

"House-leek wards off lightning. Let it stand . . ." "Our Lady's Bedstraw – stuff your pillow with it and you'll sleep like a log. Remember that. When people get old they have trouble sleeping . . ." "Feverfew brings down fever. Boil the flowers in milk and let it stand for half an hour."

She seldom ventured into the vegetable patch. On Sundays after lunch the men and the women drifted apart, blurring the division between the families. Full-skirted aunts and cousins strolled about the paths, pausing now and then to sniff the sweet-smelling pelargoniums along the way. They asked for cuttings and the grandmother was munificent. Twigs and shoots were snipped off with secateurs. Elsewhere in the garden, well hidden behind a row of bushes, she already had a bed of seedlings ready for pricking out next year, when she would impress her relatives all over again.

Over the hedge the uncles sauntered past the rows of vegetables, caps pushed back on their heads, hands in their pockets, rolled-up sleeves baring pale biceps.

"Your leeks are looking good," one of them called out, "but my peas are doing better."

"There's a fair amount of blight, Henri," another commented.

"Weak strain," he mumbled.

"Why don't you spray them?"

"No poisonous sprays in my garden!" the grandmother shouted triumphantly from among the aunts on the other side of the hedge.

"No point in spraying. A weak variety, I tell you."

One time he tried to get in her good books by sowing her name in cress along the hedge. Before the week was out the seeds had written "Andrea" in the soil. She was not overly impressed.

*

At the far end of the vegetable garden, which the grandfather had screened off from prying eyes with a row of beanstalks, rose an overgrown tangle of greenery.

"Aye-aye, what have we got here?" hooted one of the uncles. "What sort of wilderness is this?" They nudged each other. "Look, it's a right jungle . . ."

Their stomachs heaved with suppressed laughter.

The jungle was mine. One day the grandfather had given me a patch to call my own. It was the size of the dining table, partly shaded by the hedge and the rowan tree.

"We're going to do some sowing and planting, you and me," he said firmly. "I will teach you."

He raked one of the beds.

"Like so. Nice and level, like coconut matting. Watch."

He drew himself up, hugged his arms to his chest, pressed his knees together and advanced rapidly across the turned-over earth with small precise stamps of his green rubber boots, like a human steamroller.

"Our own private path," he said.

The smile he threw me then was the same routine smile he wore in the small, underexposed snapshot taken by Marcel thirty-odd years earlier. He is holding the rake upside down to draw a little furrow in the loose earth with the tip of the handle, working with the grace and concentration of a billiard player or a gondolier. He is kneeling on the loamy soil, not on the piece of old sacking he took to using in later years "against the damp". In the old days he would not have sworn as he sank to his knees, nor would he have groaned between clenched teeth: "My bones have packed up completely."

I knew the story. Bits of it had been fluttering around in my head for years. How they had beaten his kneecaps with iron pipes. How they had made him and the others hold wash tubs filled to the brim with water high over their heads, arms stretched, for hours on end. Whoever spilt a drop was whipped.

"They had it in for me, lad," he always concluded. "They had it in for me, the swine."

He fumbled in the wide pockets of his faded blue overall for a packet of seeds and tore it open. He placed one hand on the soil next to the furrow and peered in with his head close to the ground, frowning as if he were trying to read the newspaper without his glasses.

"If you just shake it gently it'll trickle out nice and even. Watch. Watch carefully now."

He grabbed me by the nape of the neck and pulled my head down until it was next to his. "See?"

I caught a whiff of old-man's breath and unshaven skin. He did not release his grasp. One hand sprinkled the seed in the furrow, the other pressed me into the line of his expectations. He drew furrows in my soul and sowed hope for something vague, not for me, but for himself.

*

"Those big white bell-flowers, Andrea," chirruped the aunts, hidden from view on the other side of the hedge, "what are they called?"

"Cape hyacinths. I can't give you cuttings. You have to grow them from seed. It takes a lot of patience, and a lot of luck. They don't normally do so well here. Too cold in winter."

The aunts nodded admiringly. The grandmother did not mention that she used seed trays in the conservatory for them to germinate during winter. Some of the aunts had conservatories, too.

"The boy will be a great gardener one day," joked the uncles. I joined in their laughter uneasily.

Ignoring me, the grandfather ushered the men towards the house.

I had planted my garden with irises and hibiscus, and had sown sunflowers. From the wet meadow verges I took wild spirea, and I bordered my allotment with tufts of lady's cushion. I laid a curving gravelled path, over which I, reduced to thumb-size in my imagination, roved through my home-made jungle.

"You ought to sow some radish seed," he said breezily, "for the kitchen. And chervil to put in the soup."

The radish I sowed was lost amid the plants already thriving. Amid the young shepherd's purse.

"Weeds!"

Amid angelica and foxglove.

"But they're flowers . . ."

He pinched the flower out of the shepherd's purse. "This stuff seeds itself all over the place."

He glanced ruefully at the rampant water-mint along the hedge.

In no time my garden acquired the shape of a horseshoe, a bastion of wild leafy growth. In that wilderness I would crouch unseen, on hot days, when my mother called my name and I wanted to be impossible to find.

"Some gardener you are," was his verdict.

The grandmother was amused by all this. A bitter contest was being fought over my head. Between his garden and hers. Between potatoes and hyacinths. The hyacinths won.

*

"My in-laws," the grandmother sometimes remarked to Stella in the sewing room, "are the kind of people who think small. Us Ornelises, we think in terms of hectares."

On Sundays she would destroy every potato shoot in sight with a jab of her heel or toe, as soon as the aunts' backs were turned. And if anyone did notice she would smile archly, saying: "Ah well, better a stray spud than a stray grenade."

Some days she was to be seen conducting a solitary inspection along the paths, her fingers black with soil. She would wipe the sweat from her forehead with the back of her hand. Crouching by the water-mint I would watch her through a gap in the hedge as she took her final turn around the garden with her bucket and trowel.

*

Years later an old photograph tumbled from the pages of a recipe book I had claimed when the house was being cleared. It shows her bending over the soil with her legs apart. Her hair is pinned back behind her ears, a few stray curls fall over her eyes. Her skirt curves up at the back, offering an unintentionally frivolous glimpse of the lace trim on a petticoat.

She glowers at the unknown person taking the picture. A stand of beech and rowan rises behind her, and I can also make out the cypress tree, still a soft-needled sapling in those days. No rose-beds. No dahlias or Cape hyacinths. Just a vast potato patch. Propped against her hip she has a wire basket full of fist-sized tubers. Her first potato crop. She had six mouths to feed while the grandfather was away in the prison camp.

CHAPTER 4

IT WAS SUNDAY, AND THE END OF MAY. THE grandmother had made boxy parcels of both the grandfather and me. She had brushed my black patent leather shoes, although my mother had done so already. The sweet stench of shoe polish wafted up my legs. She had put so much starch in the grandfather's shirt that it creaked as if it would burst every time he moved his arms.

"We've had a letter from Anna," she had told my father a few days before. "Cyriel is sick. He wants us to go and see him. I'm taking the lad along, if that's all right."

She was not seeking his opinion, merely stating her intent.

"I'm not sure . . ." my father had said. "All those old people you keep foisting on him . . ." adding, once she was out of earshot, "They fill his head with nonsense. Why can't he stay at home with his brother and sisters? They're quite happy playing in the sandpit."

For days I ran and sang in the orchard. To town. To town. She had made it sound exciting.

"I don't suppose there's any harm in it," my mother ventured. "At least it'll get him out of the house."

"If you say so." My father clenched his fists in his trouser pockets. "They act as if the boy belongs to them."

*

The grandmother buttoned my jacket, flicked the dust from my shoulders, wiped a crumb from the corner of my mouth with the tip of her handkerchief. She gave my collar a final pat, saying: "Now you wait here while I put my hat on."

Tilting her head this way and that in the oblong hall mirror she judged her appearance through narrowed eyes, bobbing and weaving to take in every detail. Her fingers flew around her hat, tucking stray locks firmly under the brim.

The grandfather, losing patience, clicked his false teeth against the roof of his mouth.

"We'll miss the train at this rate."

"There's plenty of time."

She fumbled in the pockets of her beige summer coat, seized her handbag from the chest under the mirror and rummaged in it at length.

"All the rubbish you've got there," he grinned, "all the stuff you carry around! Women! They'd take their cookers with them if they could."

She held up her purse with a sigh of relief.

*

The three of us stood side by side on the platform, keeping close to the wall.

"If an express train or a heavy steam engine comes past," the grandmother said, "you get those dangerous suction winds. That's how my father had his accident."

She squeezed my hand. I stood between her and the

grandfather. The breeze tugged at my jacket and I hopped from one foot to the other so I could see the sun glint off my patent leather toes.

The grandfather's shirt crackled. Somehow he seemed not to fill his clothes, as if he were a stowaway in a hold of pressed fabrics.

"Here it comes," he whispered. "Can you hear it? It's coming."

The electric cables over the track began to thrum softly. To town, to town.

*

Both grandparents kept their heads covered in the train. The grandfather raised his cap from time to time to mop his forehead with a handkerchief reeking of lavender. He stared fixedly out of the window.

"What's the matter with Cyriel, anyway?" he asked.

"Worn out, I expect."

She held her handbag on her lap, drumming her fingers on the large metal clasp.

"Worn out? But Cyriel isn't that old is he? Younger than I am, at any rate."

"That man wasn't cut out for hard graft with bricks and mortar. He worked himself to the bone."

"To the bone? He's a man, isn't he?"

"Cyriel had everything going for him, what with his brains. A real intellectual. Always reading. I never knew him otherwise. It was in his blood, being the son of a printer . . ."

"*I* read books too. Does that make me an intellectual?"

"Cyriel went to university. You didn't."

"University! Everybody goes to university nowadays."

"Not in his day they didn't. Cyriel could have been a professor or an engineer or an architect. Even a government minister . . ."

"A fine lot, those brainy types. If it had come to the crunch, they'd have sold us all to the Germans. Every one of us!"

"Marcel always followed his own ideals, you know that. He wouldn't have kowtowed to Hitler."

"Not him, no. Not him. What d'you think they sent him to the eastern front for? For the sake of his blue eyes? A fine lot, they were. Half of them cannon fodder, the other half in the construction industry or textile trade, if they aren't breeding cattle in the Argentine. Those chaps did very well for themselves, I tell you. Cyriel always earned good money."

The grandmother laughed disdainfully.

"Just as well Anna has her shop, though, and that her people are well off. If it wasn't for Anna the pair of them would have starved."

He fell silent. Clicked his dentures. Tapped my knee.

"Three more stops and we'll be there."

Each time the train slowed down he studied the landscape with renewed concentration and intoned the name of the next station, as though his ritual prediction were necessary for the train to come to a halt.

"Drongen next."

"Halewijn," corrected the grandmother.

"Drongen."

"Halewijn. We just passed Lauwe."

"Drongen."

The grandfather returned his gaze to the window with a shrug. The grandmother glanced at me, mouthing "Halewijn". By the time the engine driver had slammed the brakes on and a brick building with the name Halewijn in blue tiles slid into view, the stillness in the compartment had grown leaden.

*

Out on the square in front of the station there were plane trees with bicycles clustered around their trunks like helpless glistening insects that had fallen from the branches. Yellow trams swerved into the square from the side streets, screeching on their rails as though exchanging greetings in a language only trams knew. The heat shimmered above the grey asphalt. The cafés lining the square blazed in the sunlight.

"We've got time for a cup of coffee," said the grandmother. "I wouldn't mind some refreshment."

The grandfather nodded. "A cool pint would just do me nicely. Hotel Terminus, let's go there. Remember? Hotel Terminus . . ."

She did not reply, but glanced briefly in my direction. An almost imperceptible shudder passed through her body, as if she had been caught in some shameful act. It was the same shudder that I had glimpsed once before, when she heaved herself out of her chair by the sewing machine and padded to the large cupboard in her carpet slippers. She had turned the brass key with uncharacteristic circumspection and gently moved the doors to prevent the hinges from letting out a voluptuous, drawn-out squeak.

It was her custom to handle the contents of her sewing cupboard with respect, even reverence, but this time she plunged her arms in among the folded dress lengths and rolls of material with a surprising lack of decorum. The guilt-laden quiet was disturbed by plastic bags crackling surreptitiously at the back of the shelves. I heard her chewing and swallowing. She kept rustling the plastic in search of vanilla wafers, toffees or bonbons, which she devoured at great speed without any sign of enjoyment. She was quite unlike Miss Veegaete, whose entire body seemed to shrink and swell by turns, so blissfully did she savour the cake she was served on her Friday visits. The grandmother left the sewing room in a hurry, and a moment later I heard a tap running in the kitchen, as she stood by the sink sluicing away the sweetness with hastily-gulped water.

⋆

"They've papered the walls," the grandfather observed.

The hotel restaurant was chock full. Waiters bearing trays picked their way among the crowded tables. The glassed terrace overlooking the square was occupied by balding gentlemen and ladies in two-piece suits having lunch. We took a table by the window. On the glass it said *Hotel-Restaurant-Brasserie* in mirror writing. *Brasserie.*

"This place is for the top brass," the grandfather joked.

"He's having you on," said the grandmother. "Don't you listen to him . . . One coffee, a pint and an apple juice please."

The waiter scribbled on his pad and vanished as abruptly as he had appeared.

The grandparents glanced round.

"Look," the grandmother said, pointing to a blackboard over the bar indicating the day's specials. "They still do a *Soufflé Grand Marnier*."

"Mariner Puff," the grandfather said. They chuckled.

The espresso machine behind the bar squirted coffee into a jug. The grandfather laid his arms on the edge of the table and leaned forward to the grandmother.

"I can still see you sitting there."

Her eyes swept past him. "They've got new benches."

"You didn't notice me at first. Remember?"

She did not reply, but turned to me instead.

"How's your apple juice? It certainly looks good . . . This is where your grandfather and I first met."

The grandfather beamed.

"It was after the annual choir festival, 1939 as I recall. There was a big crowd, a lot of young people, everybody talking at the tops of their voices. And singing."

He sipped his pint.

"The whole square," the grandmother continued, "was decorated with flags. And the songs! Everyone joined in, didn't they? It was lovely. People used to sing real music then, there was none of that screaming and shouting you have nowadays."

"Such as the Beatles, or whatever they're called,' he said gruffly. 'How about you, lad, d'you like that kind of racket? They're not human, more like a bunch of apes if you ask me."

The grandmother began to rock gently from side to side, half humming and half singing. "When blossoming broom sets the heath ablaze."

The grandfather did not join in, which was a relief, as I had noticed the waiter giving us odd looks every time he came past.

"And gold and azure light up the days."

"They used to give us the sheet music to take home," the grandfather said. "So we could practice the songs."

"For four voices, some of them," the grandmother said, "and at the top it said how they should be sung."

She raised her forefinger. The waiter thought she was beckoning him. "With Pride and Valour, that's what it said."

The grandfather gazed dreamily out of the window at the square. "*Soufflé Grand Marnier*, I told the landlord, what's all this about *Soufflé Grand Marnier*? Have we stopped being Flemings, all of a sudden? So what do you want me to call it, he said. Simple, I said, Grand Mariner Puff, what else?"

Their shoulders shook with suppressed laughter.

"And he did change the name, too! He really did!" the grandmother said. "Once a year for the choir festival. Mariner Puff. I expect the place has changed hands by now. The old landlord probably died years ago."

"Your grandmother was sitting over there, in that corner," the grandfather said, "surrounded by young folk. Drinking a pot of Trappist. Yes, she liked her beer all right. They called her the Flower of Stuyvenerghe." He winked broadly.

"That'll do," she said. A pink flush spread over her cheeks, which was unusual.

"And that flower," the grandfather said, "was picked by me. Not that there weren't plenty of bees about. But I dare say their stings weren't as good as mine."

The grandmother set her handbag down on the table with a thump.

"I'm going to pay the bill, or we'll miss our tram."

*

The tram stopped at a crossroads on the outskirts of town. A gentle breeze ruffled the blue and white awning on a kiosk with an onion-shaped dome. The streets in this neighbourhood had a countrified air. Some of the houses were separated by yards with sheds and outbuildings that were barely visible behind tall hedges. Cherry trees poked their branches over the fence along the pavement.

Anna's shop was on the edge of the square opposite the tram shelter. A painted wooden sign over the door said "Haevermans Stationery". A display of old magazines languished alongside dusty calling cards and inkwells in the sun-drenched window. Singers with long bleached hair smiled toothily from record sleeves, which were so faded that their lips had turned green.

The grandmother gave the glass-panelled door a push. Somewhere at the back of the shop a bell shrieked, like a cat being trod on its tail. The shop was deserted, and smelt of tobacco.

The grandfather sniffed the air.

"They've got some fine little cigars here. The slender ones, good quality. Cigarillas or something. Cyriel always used to bring me some when he came to visit."

The counter on the far side of the shop was more like a cave stacked with snuff boxes, pipe heads and cigars around a cash register.

The grandmother paced the floor, took a fashion magazine from one of the shelves, glanced at the pages, replaced it and picked a few postcards out of the rack to inspect them closely.

"They're certainly taking their time," she hissed.

"This place could do with a good clean," the grandfather said.

"I'm sure Anna's got enough on her mind as it is, poor soul." The grandmother ran her fingertips over the different types of notepaper. "Mmm, paper . . ." she said, "it has such a lovely smell sometimes."

*

It was a long wait. The only sound came from the clock over the counter, crunching wearily as it struggled to make the second hand move, without success.

At long last someone could be heard thumping down a staircase in the depths of the house. A door flew open, and a gangly boy of about sixteen with a dark shadow on his upper lip and a shock of pitch-black hair appeared in the cavernous shop. He stood there looking at us blankly until his eyes widened suddenly, as if had just remembered something.

"Ah yes, of course," he muttered, tossing his head to flick the hair from his eyes and rushing out again before the grandmother had time to greet him.

"Odd chap, that," the grandfather said.

The grandmother looked down at me.

"Their youngest," she said, and then, in a low voice. "He was an afterthought, really . . ."

"*Un accident de parcours*," the grandfather said, grinning.

"Mind you, he gets good marks at school. It wouldn't hurt to follow his example."

More thumping. A woman's voice could be heard asking: "So where are they now?"

The boy growled unintelligibly.

"What's that?" cried the woman's voice. "Why didn't you ask them to come through . . ."

The door opened again and this time it was Anna who stepped into the cave.

"Fancy making Henri and Andrea wait all this time," she said with an apologetic smile. "Whatever would Cyriel say if he knew . . . Welcome. I see you've brought your grandson along."

Around her eyes lay deeply etched lines, which weren't there when she had last visited, six months earlier. The dull blond hair which had been fluffed out in a formidable perm on that occasion was now secured with old-fashioned bone combs behind her ears. She wore a grey blouse and a small pendant, which was nothing at all compared to the shiny bangles and glittery necklaces she had always worn when she came to visit. The pores of her naked skin, which would usually have been thick with makeup, now gave her features a grainy cast. When she shook my hand I saw there were tobacco stains on the tips of her index and middle finger.

"Cyriel's still asleep," she said. "Let's sit out on the veranda for a while."

At the back of the house, where the blinds had been let

down over the windows, the air was cool and funereal. The roof of the glazed veranda had been covered with linen sheets.

Anna motioned us to take a seat. The grandmother glanced round for a swift appraisal of the interior. On the windowsills stood tired house plants barely surviving in clumps of parched compost. Over the backs of the beige, fake leather chairs hung crochet antimacassars, which released little puffs of dust around our ears when we sat down. Several untidily folded newspapers littered the place.

Anna perched stiffly on a chair with a cane seat. Her fingertips kept touching the pendant on her chest.

"Well, we got here safe and sound," the grandmother remarked, for want of anything else to say.

Anna smiled feebly and turned to look at me.

"Our Wieland must show you his room later on." Over her shoulder she shouted "Wieland! What's keeping you?"

"Coming, Ma," the boy called from the kitchen. His voice was breaking, and rose from a growl to a squeak. I heard him setting cups on a tray, tipping sugar lumps into the bowl, filling the milk jug and rattling spoons in a kitchen drawer.

Anna spread her fingers on her lap and studied them at length.

"To be honest, we must be prepared for the worst."

The grandmother gave a little nod as she slipped into her tried and tested routine of bobbing her head up and down and murmuring "Yes . . . yes. I know . . . yes, yes . . . But what can you do? It's not fair, you know."

"I know," sighed Anna.

*

Meanwhile there was some commotion in the kitchen. Wieland could be heard wrestling frantically with a tightly-sealed package and, when it finally ripped open, swearing under his breath. Drawers were opened and cupboard doors slammed. Next came the sweeping sound of a brush.

Anna did not seem to notice. She raised her hands from her skirt and lowered them again.

"We're all treading on eggshells."

"As well you might be," said the grandmother. "It's very trying. Personally, I've buried more than my share . . ."

She was shocked by her own words. Her self-assured poise evaporated.

"Dear me, here I am carrying on . . . just as if . . ."

"It's no use pretending it won't happen," Anna said. "We just don't know when. It may be days or weeks, but not much longer than that. I think he knows."

Wieland came in from the kitchen carrying a tray, which he set down on the low table with a clatter. He busied himself with the distribution of cups and saucers. His Terylene flares flapped around his shins, and every few seconds he tossed the hair out of his eyes.

"If I've told him once I've told him a hundred times to get that fringe of his cut," Anna said, "but he won't listen . . ."

"It's the fashion," Wieland said, his voice switching from growl to squeak. He poured the coffee, pausing repeatedly to rub his nose with the back of his hand.

"And how's the vegetable garden, Henri?" Anna asked.

The atmosphere on the veranda lifted, to everyone's relief.

"My spuds are in a right state," the grandfather replied brightly, as if that were a good thing. "Those Colorado beetles . . . when those little blighters decide to pay you a visit . . ."

Wieland seated himself next to me on the low footstool. His body doubled up like a jackknife, with his knees almost touching his chin. He drained his cup of coffee, put it back on the table and then held his left wrist under my nose.

"Look, Our Dad's given me his watch. A proper deep sea diver's watch. Goes down to a hundred metres."

"Have you tried it yet?" I wanted to know.

The grandmother shot me a look I took to mean I should not be critical.

"I've tried diving to the bottom of the swimming pool with it. Four metres at least." After a pause he said: "And it didn't budge."

"I think I can hear him," Anna said, rising to her feet. "I'll see if he needs anything." She vanished to the back of the house.

*

The grandmother had been fidgeting with her empty coffee cup for a while before Wieland noticed. He sprang up and went round with the coffee again.

"Thank you, lad," the grandmother said. "And how's your school work?"

"Fine," Wieland said gruffly. He had no desire to pursue the subject.

"What was it you were taking your exams in? I ought to know, but I keep forgetting. At my age . . ."

"Latin," Wieland said hoarsely, "at the College of the Blessed Fathers. It's quite a long way from here."

"Latin," she sighed. "Difficult, I suppose, but worth the effort . . . Cicero, Seneca . . ." Her voice faltered as she tried to recollect. "How did it go? *Tityre, tu patulae* . . . Oh dear. *Tityre tu patulae . . . recubans* . . ." She gave up. "My memory's like a sieve . . ."

"Virgil," Wieland broke in. "A bit of a bore, to tell you the truth. Give me Caesar any day."

"What's that? *Jules César*!" The grandfather laughed. "He didn't stand for any nonsense, did he? Still, we led him quite a dance. Said so himself." He drew himself up. "Of all the Belgians, the Gauls are . . . how did it go?"

The grandmother ignored him.

Wieland filled my cup to the brim.

"I've got some great pictures upstairs," he said. "Of the army. Want to have a look?"

"He'd like that," the grandmother said.

Wieland waved his arm towards me. "Compared to my photographs," he said proudly, "even Caesar's a softie."

*

Wieland's room was seldom aired. It held all his stale breath. The orange curtains on the narrow window were half open, revealing a dusty radiator. The bed was rumpled; there were posters stuck randomly on the faded wallpaper. Wedged into a corner was a small writing table strewn with crumpled bits of paper. On the rug lay a still life of tangled shirts and underwear, all black or grey aside from the circles left behind by dried body fluids.

"It's a bit cramped in here," he said. "How d'you like my posters?"

They were too fierce-looking for my taste, but I did my best to appear enthusiastic. He had filled the spaces between the posters with pictures of pop singers in glittery outfits.

Wieland cleared away some stray clothes.

"You can sit on the bed. I've got something to show you. Some photo albums our Dad has given me. Wait."

He opened the drawer of the writing table.

I glanced round. There was a shelf of books over the bed. Most of the spines were cracked, some were so ragged that you could barely read the titles.

Onward Soldiers

All Quiet on the Western Front

Incense and Tear-gas

A thin book squeezed in between two fat volumes caught my eye. I drew it out carefully.

Pussy Street

"That one's about tarts," Wieland squeaked nervously.

His mouth was disconcertingly close to my ear. He snatched the book from me and replaced it on the shelf.

"They don't know I've got it. Come on."

He installed himself on the bed and opened a large album with a glossy black cover. More soldiers. Ramrod-straight in serried ranks, parading past the tall town houses.

"Our Dad's somewhere in there, marching with the others," Wieland said. "You just try picking him out of the crowd."

He turned the pages slowly, pausing at a picture of a mass

of men's heads, all turned toward a cluster of tiny figures on the steps of an imposing building in the distance. Above the men's heads in the foreground rose a hedge of right arms raised in diagonal salute.

"Those were the days," Wieland murmured dreamily, as if he had been there himself. He spelled out the caption: *From the steps of the Bourse, once the stronghold of Jews and plutocrats, the leader surveys his following.*

He chuckled.

"Our Dad always says, if only our people had stuck it out a bit longer, we'd all be a sight better off right now. Our Dad used to give speeches, too. They put them on records, some of them. He wouldn't let me have them, though."

He pursed his lips and whistled. "He was a quite a speaker in his day, you know."

*

Wieland's nose must have been itching again, for he squeezed his nostrils between his thumbs and rubbed up and down at length. The mattress began to heave, making some large photos spill out on the none-too-clean bedspread along with a sheaf of snapshots.

"Take a look at this. You know who they are, don't you?"

There were two men, one of whom wore an elaborate belted uniform with braiding and epaulettes, topped by an outsize military cap.

"That's our Dad," Wieland said, beaming. "Good uniform, eh? *Überscharführer*. He says it was the best time of his life."

Überscharführer.

There's no moustache, I thought, he ought to have a

moustache. I didn't know why. All I thought was: *Überscharführers* always have moustaches, and he hasn't got one. His face was very ordinary: pale, lumpy, short thick nose, eyes peering out of measly wire-framed spectacles. A shopkeeper in fancy dress.

I swallowed hard and glanced at Wieland.

He grinned. The downy black hairs on his upper lip lay in perfectly regimented lines.

"And that one there," he said. "You know who that is, don't you?"

Next to the shopkeeper in disguise stood a slim figure in a dark, unshowy uniform. Instinctively I blurted: "It's Marcel."

"Our Dad always says Marcel could have gone far. He could have done a lot to help the Flemish cause. It's a shame he died before . . ."

Wieland shut the album, jumped up and put it back in the drawer.

Silence fell. I just sat there, stroking the bedspread.

He watched me narrowly.

"Great pictures, eh?"

"Yes, yes."

He sprawled on the bed again, letting his hand rest chummily on my shoulder. "I know what people say behind our backs. Do they call you 'blackshirt' at your school too?"

He didn't wait for me to reply.

"Mind you, I couldn't care less . . . Come on, let's be blackshirts and talk about girls." He wrinkled his nose. "You got a girlfriend?"

I stammered non-committally.

"I suppose not. They're always a bit backward in the country . . . I've got one, though."

"What's her name?"

"Kathy." His voice cracked again. He jiggled his right foot and tossed the lock of hair from his forehead for the umpteenth time.

"Wouldn't it be a good idea to get your hair cut sometime?" I asked, to change the subject. "It keeps getting in your eyes."

"Girls are crazy about long hair," he boasted. "Wait. I'll show you a picture of Kathy."

He sat up and raised his right arm to the bookshelf over the bed. His hand fumbled around, tipping a tin soldier onto his pillow, followed by a stamp bearing a postmark and a revolting crumpled handkerchief. He drew himself up further, lost his balance and fell on top of me. His dark jersey gave off a metallic body smell. I tried to push him off.

"Sorry," he stammered. It sounded a little too studied.

His bony hands gripped my shoulders.

"Let me go, runt."

He flattened me against the mattress, drew himself up again and planted his knees on my upper arms. His trousers crackled with static.

His face broke into a hard smile. "See if you can escape now."

He took a deep breath and looked around with a show of unconcern.

"What shall we do? Any ideas? D'you know how to snog?"

I wasn't sure I knew what he was getting at.

"Snog. Don't you understand?"

He leaned over until his nose touched mine and his fringe tickled my eyelashes. His eyes were dark brown.

"Snog," he repeated.

He put his lips to my right ear.

"What girls do. Not like this . . ." he said, moving his lips to my cheek, " . . . like this."

He pressed his face down and ground his mouth against mine to force it open. I screwed up my eyes and clenched my jaws. His tongue wormed itself between my lips. Our teeth collided painfully.

He shrank back and wiped his lips with the back of his hand.

"Pig."

He leaned forward for a renewed attempt. Suddenly his mother's voice called from the landing: "Wieland!"

We drew back instantly and glared at each other from opposite sides of the bed.

"Wieland?" Anna repeated.

She pushed the door open a little way, eyed the pair of us carefully, put on a solemn expression and said: "Our Dad, Wieland, would like you to take a nice photo of us all." She paused. "You know where the camera is."

Wieland left the room. His mother motioned me to follow her.

"He didn't try to tie you up, I hope," she said. "He keeps wanting to play Red Indians. His friends don't fancy it, so they've stopped coming to the house. All of seventeen and still playing games."

Shaking her head she retreated to the sparsely-lit landing.

*

Cyriel was sitting in the biggest chair on the veranda, with cushions at his back and a tartan rug over his legs, which were propped up on the footstool Wieland had occupied before. He was wearing spectacles; the frames were slightly heavier than in the photograph taken forty years ago. The lenses enlarged his eyes in their deep sockets, making him look like an old carp gasping for breath.

The grandmother inclined her head sideways to catch what he was saying. I saw her stuffing a sheaf of papers into her handbag just as I came into the room.

"I kept them all for you," I heard Cyriel say. His voice came in weak little gasps. Under his chin the flaccid skin sagged over his Adam's apple, which rose with each laboured swallow to vanish into the wrinkles for a long time. Out of each nostril came a plastic tube connected to an oxygen cylinder suspended from a metal frame behind his chair.

"You should have them, they're no use to Anna . . . His last letters . . . I still can't read them without . . . You're a strong woman, Andrea . . ."

The grandmother's chin started to tremble and her lips were nowhere to be seen, the way they were early in the morning when her false teeth were still in their glass by the tap and she went about the house in her quilted dressing gown, her slippers flip-flopping on the floor. They were like camels' feet in the sand. She even had a camel's hump. When her shoulders sloped forward her spine made a bump between her shoulder blades. Without her false teeth she seemed quite desiccated. Her face would shrivel up, as though the water reservoir in her hump had run dry.

Cyriel had heard me come in. He turned his head in my direction and extended his hand. His fingers were bony and wide at the tips. They looked like drumsticks.

"Ha, the young grandson!"

I could feel the tremor in his fingers when he shook my hand.

He looked up at the grandmother, who was putting her handbag down at her feet.

"Marcel to a tee . . ."

"He's inherited his mother's eyes," she said, "but for the rest – an out-and-out Ornelis."

Cyriel turned to me again. "So you'll be another staunch Fleming, will you?"

"That depends," the grandmother said.

*

In the meantime Wieland had appeared with the camera, an unwieldy contraption in a dark leather case.

"I suppose I'll have to use the flash," he said eagerly, fitting a fresh film into the slot. "The sun's gone now, and there's not much light here because of the sheets on the roof."

Mechanically, as if he were loading a gun, he clicked an outsize metal disc onto the camera. He held it up against his nose and stepped around the veranda like an automated Cyclops.

"Must find the best angle."

The grandfather rose from his chair. "Quite an old model, isn't it?"

"Never gave me any trouble . . ." Cyriel gasped. "Bought it in Cologne . . . Made in Germany, never wears out . . ."

"And then they say Germany lost the war!" Anna chimed in. "You should see their industry. All those factories . . ."

"You've all got to move a bit closer together," Wieland instructed, posting himself in a corner of the veranda.

The grandfather stood next to Anna on one side of Cyriel's chair. The grandmother hovered on the other side with me planted in front of her. All of us focused on Wieland's Cyclopean lens. Cyriel crossed his arm over his chest to hide the oxygen tube.

Wieland was clearly enjoying himself.

"Now if you all say cheese," he cried, "then you'll look as if you're laughing . . . One . . . Two . . ."

"Never mind about that," Anna said, "what's there to laugh about, anyway?"

The whoosh of an umbrella bursting open was followed by a blinding light.

*

Six weeks later the photograph was prominently displayed in the grandmother's glass-fronted cabinet, at the foot of the Yser Tower. We are all on it, white-faced, as though the flash had drained the blood from our veins.

The funeral mass was attended by a crowd of boys in short trousers. They stood in the nave swinging Flemish Lion flags so vigorously that they churned up a strong breeze. Wieland, with bowed head, shuffled in the wake of his elder brothers and sisters behind the coffin. Our eyes met briefly. There was no flicker of recognition as he set his features in an expression of dramatic grief. His mother must have got her way in the end, for he had had a haircut. His jet-black hair was much shorter now, although still long enough for him to toss it out of his eyes.

*

"Sad, very sad" was the only thing the grandmother said all the way home. Her handbag bulged with the papers Cyriel had given her. I had seen them when Wieland took the photograph: a thick wad of envelopes, yellowed and frowsty-looking, slit along the top.

Arriving home the grandmother left her handbag on the chest in the hall as usual. She took her coat off, helped the grandfather out of his, hung both coats on a hanger and disappeared into the parlour.

"He's had it," I heard the grandfather say, before the door shut behind them.

The grandmother went to the kitchen to make supper. I could hear her banging cupboard doors.

The handbag stood on top of the chest. All I needed to do was reach out my hand – one of the envelopes was sticking out. I drew it out between thumb and forefinger.

The beams of the house stretched and settled plaintively in the heat of the summer afternoon. She, who otherwise heard everything, heard nothing now. She rattled the pans and filled the kettle.

I undid a few buttons and slipped the envelope inside my shirt.

Upstairs, in the attic, I spread the letter out flat. The pencil had faded with the years, and the spidery handwriting was hard to read. It said something about tomatoes being "wonderful here. Four, five kilograms per plant, and as sweet as apples."

What fascinated me most of all was the great bird on the outside, with its curved beak, strong talons, spreading tail feathers. Miss Veegaete would love it.

CHAPTER 5

THE DRESS WAS ALMOST READY. THE BUTTONS STILL needed to be sewn on and it had not been pressed yet, but it hung grandly on its hanger against the wardrobe door. In the gathering gloom of the sewing room it was like a deserted fortress looming up out of the clutter of fashion magazines, bolts of material and dress patterns. Putting my head under the skirt and just standing there in the purple sheen was enough to make me feel as if I were Miss Veegaete herself, large and bloated, bosoms and all.

Evening rolled down the attic stairs, percolated into the corners of the rooms, trickled imperceptibly down the walls, robbing the furniture of its colours, its distinctive features, and eventually its contours. Miss Veegaete's dress became a capacious, floating shadow pressing up against its alter ego in the wardrobe mirror. Dress and mirror image seemed to hug one another in the night, two wavering silhouettes in search of a body.

The grandmother had sent me off to bed early as usual, and as usual I had crept out from the covers within the hour. The evening freshness cooled the roof, which gave out a surprisingly loud salvo of clicks. As the night wore on a soughing sound ran through the rafters, as if the house were sagging into a leisurely pose. Stella would be doing the same at this hour. After supper she hung her apron among the dishcloths in the kitchen and withdrew to listen to her radio: a soft male voice burbling genteelly from her room.

At the end of the corridor the door to the parlour was ajar: a dark slab with light around the edges. Tiptoeing into the beam, I was able to see the grandmother sitting at one end of the table. All I could see of the grandfather through the crack was his elbow resting on the tabletop.

I moved closer. The grandmother was wearing her reading glasses. She was holding one of the letters Cyriel had given her. The others lay in a pile between her and the grandfather.

I saw her lips move, but could not hear what she was saying. She must have been speaking in a low whisper. They always kept their voices down after I had been sent to bed. She was reading aloud, and as she read I saw her nod her head. Her eyebrows shot up intermittently, and I could hear the grandfather's little grunt at the end of each sentence, indicating that she could proceed. When she faltered I knew it was because he was interrupting her. I saw him clench and unclench his fist.

The grandmother shook her head vigorously, paused a while and then went on nodding. The grandfather's hand rose up above the tabletop, as if he were addressing an invisible third party occupying the chair opposite him. His hand reached out two or three times, at which the grandmother shook her head with mounting agitation.

"That's not true, and you know it . . ."

Her voice faded.

"What does it matter," I heard him say. His hand stopped moving.

They fell silent.

Then the grandmother resumed her reading, only to raise her eyes from the letter almost immediately.

"A lot," she blurted, in a surprisingly loud voice, which evidently shocked her, too. "It matters a lot," she continued, sinking to a whisper, "to me." She patted her chest with her left hand. "A lot."

She replaced the letter in its envelope, which she laid down on her right before taking a new one from the pile.

She read aloud for the next hour or so, working her way steadily through the pile of letters, spreading them out flat, folding them again and adding them to the slowly growing pile to her right. Now and then a fresh disagreement flared up, which soon subsided.

Finally all the letters were in the pile on her right. She took off her glasses and rubbed her eyes. I heard the scrape of a chair as the grandfather rose to his feet. I strained to hear whether he was heading for the door, my mind racing with calculations as to how long it would take me to hide on the stairs to the attic.

*

The attic – where the raincoats of the dead in their mahogany wardrobe would have melted into the inky blackness by now. So would the great-grandmother's astrakhan coat, which Stella slipped off its hanger when she thought she was alone. It reached almost to her ankles, and the sleeves were far too long for her short arms. She wrapped it tightly around her body, turned her back to the wardrobe mirror and twisted round to see how it looked, gauging how much she would have to take it in at the waist for it to fit snugly around the hips. She studied the angle of the collar on her chest, shook the lapels, did up buttons and undid them again, judging the effect all the while with darting, beady eyes.

"Stella puts Oda's coat on sometimes," I tittle-tattled one day, when she and the grandmother were standing at the kitchen table sifting flour. I felt guilty immediately.

Stella blushed bright red and shot me a searing look. For a time the only sound was the soft slap of her hands on the dough.

The grandmother stood with her back to us rinsing a saucer under the tap.

She was taking her time. She placed the saucer in the rack, dried her hands on her apron, sat down, rolled up a sheet of kitchen foil with a nonchalant air and then said sharply: "She's not the only one . . ."

Her words plunged a dagger in my ribs. I cringed.

"What grown-ups do is their own business," she went on. "If they want to act the *madame*, it's entirely up to them."

Stella stopped kneading abruptly, her hands lay still in the bowl with dough as though she had suddenly decided to become a house plant.

"But every self-respecting housewife knows she ought to dust her paws with flour first. Stops the dough from sticking."

All three of us seemed to freeze into a *tableau vivant*, until a moment later the grandmother turned to the sink again and Stella went back to slapping her dough. I was reminded of a herd of elephants sloshing across a muddy pool.

*

It was only by magic that she could have found me out. I had put everything back in the old travelling trunk exactly as I had found it. Socks on top, in bundled pairs. Underneath were the trousers with their sickly-sweet smell of camphor and dust. Under the trousers were the three shirts. Two grey, one checked. At the bottom lay school textbooks and exercise books, with much-thumbed labels. Marcel Ornelis. Class C. Saint Laurens. Inside were stock-raising techniques, domestic fowl and cattle breeds, irrigation methods, with pencilled scribbles in the margin, faint from being erased: *Fly Bluefoot fly!! All hail to Flanders!*

The shirts did not match the picture in my mind's eye, which was of a slim figure, military, clean-cut. A dark shape scissored out of the night. The check shirt had a peasant collar. He must have worn it buttoned up to the top, the same way it now lay folded in the trunk. He may have rolled up the sleeves on hot days. Up to the elbows, or over them. Probably over.

Glory to our Flemish Heroes!

He would have pencilled his slogans in secret, hiding behind the boys in the row in front. Perhaps he had shielded what he was writing with his left hand. He would have rubbed them out himself, later on. Possibly at the behest of a teacher. Or he might have been afraid, or ashamed, as if he had scrawled an obscenity on the wall of one of the lavatories. The older boys sometimes did this, even in Miss Veegaete's lavatory. She would sweep out of her palatial privy seething with indignation, an empress stepping onto her balcony to face the rebellious rabble below.

Every single item had been replaced in the trunk in the correct sequence, for hadn't I had plenty of practice observing the strictest order each Friday anew, portrait after portrait? I had even dusted the lid with my handkerchief so as to remove any fingerprints. Perhaps I had been too fastidious. Perhaps I had made the trunk look suspiciously spic and span. Now, in the early hours of the night, it would be filling up with black water, up to the brim and over, like an overflowing bathtub.

*

The grandfather switched the light off over the sofa. The grandmother folded her glasses and put them in their case. I sloped back to my room and drew the cold sheets up to my chin.

The familiar sounds of their nightly ritual wafted towards me. A Steradent tablet fizzing in a glass on the bathroom shelf. The splash of water on their faces, hands, wrists, while they grinned toothlessly in the stillness. The creaking of their joints, or it could have been the lining of their slippers, as they shambled down the corridor. The grandfather checked all the rooms, opening doors, glancing inside, and shutting them again. By the time he reached my door I was lying on my side, breathing through parted lips with studied regularity.

I knew without opening my eyes that he was standing in the doorway with his hand on the doorknob and his mouth twisted into an involuntary rictus. His flabby lips made soft smacking sounds. Finally he shut the door. A moment later their bedsprings groaned weakly under their combined weight.

*

I had learned to keep my mouth shut about the footsteps in the dead of night. I had mentioned them only once.

"You've got too much imagination, you have," she had said. "You've got so much imagination it doesn't fit inside your head. It'll be the pigeons you can hear. Or your grandfather, when he goes to the lavatory."

His footfall was familiar to me. He favoured his left foot to spare his bad knee. Hard-soft, hard-soft came the creak of his slippers, or was it his joints, as he headed to the bathroom and back again.

Perhaps she was right. It would be the pigeons – they certainly behaved as if they carried on until late at night. All the other birds would be up and about by sunrise, while the pigeons spent half the morning perching side by side on the gutter, a row of befuddled feathery balls on little legs. All that was missing were ice packs on their heads. They were the culprits – but then again maybe they were not. The veils of the night were more than a match for common-sense explanations.

*

Moonlight seeped through the slit under the door toward the bedstead. From the sewing room it inched across the corridor as the night took its course. First it cast a long sliver of light on the floor, then receded slowly, blurring the space.

Miss Veegaete's dress dangling against the wardrobe door would be all silvery by now, but I did not dare sneak inside to take a look. The attic had come alive. The rafters creaked from one end of the house to the other. I told myself it was the pigeons.

Outside, the neighbours' dog barked at the stars and rattled its bowl. It was a bad-tempered, ugly creature, but I was grateful for the noise.

The night wore on. The cold rose up from the ground, penetrating the walls. The atmosphere was rife with little ticks and sighs; the kitchen utensils seemed to be vying for space, clicking and rattling like so many blackbirds singing to claim their territory. The moon was setting, and in the attic an inky blackness started pouring from all the cupboards and chests, cascading down the stairs. I couldn't see a thing. All around me the dark pressed up against the walls, rustling behind cupboards and nibbling at the woodwork. Rats or mice behind the skirting boards. Perhaps.

I considered my options: count up to ten thousand, say, or do some more praying, or pretend that fairies really existed and I could make any wish I pleased. What if it worked? What if all the stuff that fell off the table were to band together? A strip of suede. A tuft of fur. What if all the snippets of serge joined forces with a couple of buttons? They could enlist the tangle of basting threads on the floor, and bribe a dozen thimbles while they were at it. They could invade the table drawer and conspire with the lame zippers. Murder in reverse. A new perspective. A more bearable tomb. So he would stop roaming the house in his stockinged feet, all the way from attic to basement, pausing at my door, deathly quiet, jealous of me – Marcel to a tee but for the eyes which I got from my mother. Until finally I was numbed by sleep and my head dropped like the lid on the travelling trunk.

CHAPTER 6

THE GRANDMOTHER AND I TOOK THE BACK LANE TO the village, walking in the shade of the poplar trees. June was drawing to a close. The languid foliage presaged the monotony of the long school holidays. Miss Veegaete's new dress had been carefully folded and wrapped by the grandmother.

The whole morning had been taken up with last-minute preparations. This had nothing to do with the dress, which was ready – it was the grandmother who had to prepare herself. Stella put curlers in her mistress's hair, row upon row of them until she looked like an old-fashioned judge with a sausage wig. The grandmother sat unmoved on her chair by the window throughout, taking no notice of the bustle while she looked through the post and read the paper.

Stella covered the grandmother's head with an elasticated cap made of white nylon; at the top it was joined to a flaccid tube that was connected with the vacuum cleaner.

The grandmother raised her hands briefly to feel whether the cap was properly in place and gave a little nod. Stella swaggered over to the vacuum cleaner and pressed the switch with a flourish, as if it were a new type of rocket she was launching.

The machine let out a roar. The nylon tube stiffened. The cap ballooned.

"Warm enough?" Stella shouted over the din. "Not too hot?"

The grandmother said no. She was like a cave painting, a prehistoric fertility goddess with a ceremonial headdress.

The vacuum cleaner roared non-stop for the next quarter of an hour. The grandmother's head emerged from the dryer steaming like a freshly baked cake. Stella pulled out the rollers, dragged a hairbrush through the stiff curls, and misted the sculpted tresses in enough hairspray to glue the flies to the ceiling.

"Remember, now," the grandmother admonished, "you must mind your manners. No more than two biscuits – if we are offered any, that is. Or just one piece of cake. And don't go butting in when the grown-ups are talking. Understand?"

"OK!"

"OK, OK . . . why don't you just say 'yes'. All these new-fangled words. What's wrong with Flemish anyway? People even say 'sorry' nowadays, as if they're English. Sorry indeed. I used to have a dog called Sorry."

"Yes Grandma."

She went off to put on her smartest outfit, for which she had chosen the material and cut with the greatest care. Needless to say it was less ostentatious than her creation for Miss Veegaete, which was lying in the parcel on the chest.

*

Miss Veegaete lived at the end of the village in an unassuming brick house on a street corner. On one side it adjoined the school playground, on the other there was a drive with linden trees, a green tunnel that led to the gates of the castle.

"Well now, so it's quite finished, is it?" trilled Miss Veegaete, seeing the parcel when she answered the door.

Miss Veegaete's house did not have a hall, which always struck me as odd. A house without a hall was too eager, somehow, and there was an unseemly intimacy about it. Looking past Miss Veegaete's ample shoulders you could see straight into her living room. The wallpaper was patterned with clouds of lilies and foliage bursting forth from curvaceous urns, which seemed intent on drawing the eye away from the framed still lifes with game. Fancy china, charming pendules, weather houses, almanacs and shepherdesses of fine biscuit porcelain cluttered every surface in sight. The whole mass of bric-a-brac was a twinkling avalanche gradually encroaching on the backs of the heavily patterned settees. Next to the piano stood a spindly wrought iron birdcage, from which a pair of parakeets raised a neurotic outcry at the intrusion.

Something moved in the background, and it was only then that I noticed Miss Veegaete's brother. He was lounging on one of the settees watching television.

"Afternoon, afternoon," he mumbled in a nasal voice, without taking his eyes off the screen.

"Our Norbert and his telly," said Miss Veegaete. "It's cycle racing from morning till night in this house."

"It's the Tour de France," Norbert protested. "I can't miss that."

"I watch it myself, now and then," said the grandmother.

"Not for the sport, really, but because the scenery is so pretty sometimes. The French certainly know how to attract tourists."

Miss Veegaete took the parcel from the grandmother, laid it down on a chair and fumbled with the wrapping.

"Oh my dear Andrea," she cried, pulling the dress up by the shoulders and holding it at arms' length. "How very nice it looks! I'll put it on later, but let's have a little treat first. Our Louise has been baking."

At that very moment Louise, Miss Veegaete's elder sister, kicked the scullery door open and came in bearing an impressive pastry construction. It was a tall cylinder with icing on top sprinkled with chopped hazelnuts, and it seemed to me nigh on impossible that she could have made it herself. She made me think of a tree which had started out with the potential for shooting up tall and slender but which had since, being confined between two rocks, lost all sense of direction. Just above her hips her spine canted forward at an alarming angle, then arched back up to the shoulders, where it lurched forward again.

Louise seemed about to collapse on top of the table, cake and all. The cups shivered in their saucers.

"Ah, a proper *millefeuille*," the grandmother said reverently. "You need a lot of patience for that sort of pastry. I seldom do it. All that rolling out, folding over, rolling again. Not my cup of tea."

"Actually," Louise squeaked, " I love keeping busy in my little kitchen."

Her voice box had been invaded by a frightened bird which

had clipped its own wings. "And little Linda here has been a great help."

I had failed to notice that Louise had not emerged from the scullery alone. Little Linda skipped across the tiles and around the table. She halted right under my nose. A wisp of a girl; fey, fair-haired, almost translucent. Her lace-trimmed frock looked as if it was made of spun sugar.

"*Dans ma pochette j'ai beaucoup d'argent Italien*," little Linda shrilled. She threw me a saccharine smile, unaware that her tongue was sticking out. Her front teeth were missing.

"My niece," explained Miss Veegaete, brimming with emotion.

"Her *Papa* and *Maman* are on holiday, which is why little Linda has come to stay with us. The country air will do her good. She often comes to take a cure *chez nous campagnards*, don't you *ma petite*?"

Little Linda was too busy radiating self-satisfaction to reply.

The grandmother nudged me to shake hands with her.

I did not move a muscle.

Little Linda tapped my left shoulder with her forefinger and giggled with her tongue hanging out, "*Enchantée, campagnard*!"

"They're ever so quick to learn, these modern youngsters," Miss Veegaete said, laughing.

"Hullo," I said gruffly.

Little Linda sauntered back to the table.

*

The *millefeuille* turned out to be a horrendously frustrating delicacy that crumbled into nothing under my fork. Fortunately Louise had spread a generous filling of *crème au beurre* halfway down the layers of flaky pastry.

Little Linda sat on a chair wedged in between her two aunts. She stared in front of her with a self-possessed air, not deigning to look at her plate.

"*Tu n'aimes pas*?" Miss Veegaete inquired anxiously. They conversed almost inaudibly, in little staccato squeaks. From somewhere in their heads they transmitted thought waves, which only they could receive, not I.

"*Non*," mewed little Linda. She pouted, putting her hands on her stomach.

Silently Miss Veegaete reached for little Linda's plate and tipped the slice of cake onto her own plate.

"Not yet six years old and already a real *Bruxelloise*, that child," said Louise with thinly concealed disapproval. "Airs and graces *à volonté*."

"She's a bundle of nerves, poor lamb," Miss Veegaete said quietly, so that little Linda would not hear. "Things are a bit strained over there."

"I knew from the start," said Louise. "That woman, with all her tricks, she's not right for our Antoine. He likes the country. Drives the poor chap up the wall, being stuck in that flat in Brussels."

"Damn . . ." said Miss Veegaete's brother.

The television rumbled and choked as though fighting down a sneezing fit. The screen filled with wavy stripes.

"And just during the sprint, too," he moaned. "Damn . . ."

"Norbert!" Miss Veegaete said sharply.

The television let out a dying wheeze, at which the picture changed to a snowstorm.

"Right, that just about finishes it," growled Norbert.

He got up, flung his newspaper on the settee, switched the television off and came to sit at table with the rest of us.

"I might as well have a piece of that *gâteau* now."

Louise cut him a slice.

"Indeed my lad," said Miss Veegaete with a glance in my direction, "you'll be in Master Norbert's class soon. Just a few more days and it'll be time for you and me to say goodbye."

"Oh dear," the grandmother replied, "he does so like his Miss."

Little Linda gave a scornful chuckle. "*Pauvre petit* . . ."

"Did you hear that!" Miss Veegaete tittered. "So amusing!"

*

Master Norbert could very well have done with two chairs. The one he sat on struggled valiantly to support his rear, but was unable to suppress the occasional mild groan. Master Norbert's torso seemed intent on annexing his head. It would not be long before there was barely a dent to separate the two.

"He's a fine reader, this little chap," said Miss Veegaete, "but his arithmetic isn't as good as it should be."

" 'Rithmetic," cried Master Norbert, "I'll teach him 'rithmetic. Once I get my hands on him he'll be doing sums like a cashier. Multiplication tables in the morning. Divisions in the afternoon. He'll be up to his eyes in 'rithmetic."

Master Norbert's glasses were so heavily framed I could not tell if it was me he was looking at. I prayed it was not. The look in his eyes told of a fathomless lassitude, against which I rebelled quite spontaneously two months later. I became an expert in long division.

He was the monstrous antithesis of his sister. They had to be identical twins, that was it, and all the spite, all the loutishness had collected in him. I often saw his grey-coated figure shambling across the playground. On sunny days when the windows were open his dull cleric's voice could be heard all over the school intoning, "In the name of the Father, the Son and the Holy Ghost, amen," with his pupils falling in after a two-syllable delay. His geography lessons consisted of indicating the different countries on the maps above the blackboard with a long pointer.

" 'Rithmetic and the regions of Belgium, that's good mental exercise . . . polders, coastal regions . . ."

This time I knew it was me he was looking at.

"There's Haspengouw, where they grow juicy pears . . . and the Condroz, where the cattle are sleek and the girls as creamy as farm butter."

He thought he was very witty. His laughter was an earthquake, with his navel marking the epicentre.

"And all of that together, that's Belgium for you. Flemings and Walloons under one king and crown." He dropped his hands wearily on the table. "Fat lot of good it did us," he muttered.

*

There was still at least a quarter of the *millefeuille* left when Louise disappeared with it into the kitchen, leaving me not only with a hollow feeling in my stomach but also at the mercy of Master Norbert.

Miss Veegaete and the grandmother had gone upstairs, and little Linda had skipped along at their heels without any objections being raised. I could hear them talking and thumping about overhead. Miss Veegaete would have slipped on her dress by now and be striking balletic poses in front of the mirror. What else could be setting the chandelier over the table so ecstatically atremble? I felt cruelly excluded. I had observed Miss Veegaete in her new dress just once, but at that stage the segments were still loosely stitched together, giving her a higgledy-piggledy, Frankenstein-like look.

Master Norbert inserted his thumb halfway into his mouth to scrape the back of his teeth, pulling a face like a gargoyle on the flying buttress of a Gothic church. His unshaven cheeks and moustache shrouded the bottom half of his face in darkness. His stomach gave out regular rumbles, as though the triumphant ingestion of all that cake and coffee were only now being celebrated.

I was awestruck. He would obliterate me, I was sure. Shatter everything that was mine. Wring the life out of me and smother me with his bulbous mass. I felt a blind rage well up inside me and longed desperately to turn to stone there and then, a solid rock of granite capable of withstanding the force of hammers, chisels and files.

Master Norbert collected the spittle in his mouth and pushed it out between his front teeth with the tip of his tongue. There was no trace of embarrassment. He was fossilised in his habits. He was a great big rock himself, one of those erratic boulders that found their way here when the ice cap melted millions of years ago. He had come inching southwards, inexorably, smugly, flattening everything in his path. I could picture him heaving into the classroom, and there was no doubt in my mind that he would pull hairs out of his nostrils and lick up earwax from the ball of his thumb, which he'd hold under his nose first, of course, to smell the gobbets.

From the depths of his gut rose a bubble of gas. It burst in his throat with a dry pop followed by a burbling sound, like a barrel of cider being uncorked in the cellar.

It was not long before Louise returned from doing the dishes in the kitchen, for which I was deeply grateful. She was wearing an apron, and there were suds on her wrists.

Before taking her seat at the table she raised her fingers to her temples. It was only then that I noticed she wore a wig. She turned to address me.

"All this time I've been wondering," she said in her squeaky voice, "who the little chap might be, the one who's always by himself. I see you every day, you know, from my kitchen window. You don't play marbles. You don't join in with the others. You don't play Cowboys and Indians. Just as well, too, I'd say. All those nasty guns going bang bang bang . . ."

"Takes after Marcel, he does," growled Norbert.

By the time Louise came into the room he had terminated his tooth-cleaning session, much to my relief.

"Marcel always kept to himself, too."

"But his heart was in the right place," said Louise, "and he had a wonderful singing voice. Goodness me, how that boy could sing. How about you, can you sing well? Marcel was a right nightingale."

"A right idealist, too. Perhaps too much so . . ." Norbert opined. He could not resist the temptation to stick his pinkie in his ear and give it a little twist.

"Not like you, eh," grinned Louise. "Always making a run for it, you were. They probably needed special bullets to keep up with you."

Norbert's cheeks reddened. A fresh eruption announced itself in his intestinal tract. He tilted his chair back and stabbed the air with his forefinger.

"And I'd do a runner all over again, Goddammit! What d'you take me for? Some poor sod cowering in a trench? Convenient, that – all they'd need to do is shovel some earth on top. For Flanders, they told us. To battle! I'd do a runner, that's for sure . . ."

"You wouldn't have lasted more than two seconds before dropping dead like a stuck pig," Louise chuckled. "We're getting on, Norbert. Rickety farm carts, all three of us."

Norbert calmed down. His eyes were fixed on mine, and his expression softened. "Let's hope he'll have some gumption, if it ever happens again." His voice took on an unexpectedly fatherly tone. "If I had a boy of my own and all that stuff and nonsense started up again, I'd keep him chained up in the cellar. Well, it's all in the past now, what's done is done."

He retreated into silence. Footsteps thumped down the stairs.

"And so," cooed Miss Veegaete as she swept into the room, "we're all prepared to brave the cold of winter. Such a nice new ensemble. How much do I owe you, Andrea, do tell me . . ."

She took out her purse. Little Linda skipped out from behind her back and climbed onto a chair. She wore hair clips in the shape of jaunty ladybirds with big spots on their backs. The sight of them did not make me like her any better.

*

Linda came to the grandmother's house only once. Miss Veegaete brought her along when she paid her autumn visit to discuss her spring wardrobe.

While Miss Veegaete's measurements were being taken I lured little Linda to the attic, to show her my lair, my secret hiding place behind a forgotten dresser, an old armchair and the suitcase stocked with goodies I had filched piecemeal from the cupboard in the sewing room.

I offered her a big sweet with a runny filling.

"*Très jolie*," she murmured.

"*Regarde moi*," I said, "this is how you're supposed to eat it."

I bit into the side of the sweet and sucked out the blood-red syrupy filling.

"Go on, you try . . ."

Little Linda took a bite. The filling spilled from her lips and trickled down her chin. Next thing her face was covered in sticky goo and she was looking around anxiously for something to wipe her hands on. Before she knew it the goo was dripping from her chin onto her dazzling white blouse.

She stared at me, wide-eyed. Not in anger, not in dismay, but in sheer panic. I felt a stirring of sympathy. I pictured her, trembling like a leaf in the Brussels flat while her *Papa* and her *Maman* made a scene.

She held out her arms sideways, as if I had nailed her to an invisible cross.

"*Tu . . . vous . . .*" she faltered.

Dear me, how upset Miss Veegaete would be when she saw the mess her little china doll had made of herself!

Little Linda's face turned red. Her hands fluttered about helplessly, her sky-blue eyes filled with tears and her mouth was set in a grimace. The red filling oozed from the corners of her lips. She did not make much of a noise, other than a hoarse sort of whistling. Then she clutched her stomach and doubled up, sobbing. I felt like a monster.

*

"You came on foot," Miss Veegaete remarked as she let us out. Little Linda lolled against her aunt's legs.

"We thought we'd take a stroll along the fields," the grandmother said. "Saves meeting all the local worthies."

"I know what you mean," said Miss Veegaete. "Would you believe it, Andrea, I can still see the spite on their faces. I can always tell how they felt about the blackshirts, even if I've never set eyes on them before. It's written all over them."

"It's time they stopped picking on us," said the grandmother. "All those last-minute heroes, yes indeed, once the Germans had gone it was fine for them to be brave. I can still hear them marching up the drive in their shiny boots . . . inspection for this, inspection for that. Whether I charged fixed prices. Whether I kept the books in order . . . it got to the point where I suffered stomach cramps when the milkman came to the gate . . . But we must be off now."

"Don't forget, *jeune homme*," Miss Veegaete called after me, "that we're going to do something special on our last day of term. You won't forget, will you?"

I nodded.

"The boys are going to give their own lessons," Miss Veegaete explained, "about the animal kingdom."

"Ah well, that won't be a problem then," replied the grandmother. "He spends all his time in the fields. He knows exactly where the ducks' nests are."

"All the better," laughed Miss Veegaete. "It'll be most instructive, I'm sure."

"*Au revoir, campagnard,*" little Linda simpered.

The door closed.

"Well," said the grandmother, "they do like showing off their French, don't they?"

*

It was nearly dusk and clouds were gathering. The soft blue sky faded into swathes of pearl-grey. A brassy, menacing glow rose up behind the poplar trees, and from the horizon came the rumble of thunder.

"It looks like we're in for a real downpour," the grandmother said, glancing up at the clouds accusingly. She hastened her pace and hurried me along.

The first drops were plopping onto the sandy garden path when we reached the gate. A gust of wind tore at the crowns of the apple trees. She had hardly flung the front door open when the rain came down in torrents.

"Just in time! That was lucky."

The first flash of lightning reduced her, for a fraction of a second, to a two-dimensional, dark shape in the hall. It had luminous hair.

Stella and the grandfather were sitting in the parlour playing cards.

"There you are at last!" he cried. "I'm sick and tired of gin rummy. It's a game for milksops. At least we can play hearts now."

He shuffled the cards and cut them in four stacks.

Stella got up to unplug the wireless from the wall socket. "I'm not too fond of thunderstorms," she said.

Meanwhile the rain gushed down the roof, overflowing the gutters.

The grandfather made a fan of his cards.

"Come on, what's keeping you?" he said brusquely, drumming his fingers on the table.

"I'm putting my money away," she called from the kitchen.

"I don't fancy lightning much either," Stella said.

There was a loud crash of thunder.

"That was close!" Stella crossed herself. "The worst thing about stormy weather is that I always get this pain in my side. I wasn't bothered when I was younger. Now I get this pain every single time. And when it hits me here," she said, pointing to her hip, "then I know we're in for a thunderstorm. Without a doubt."

"It's the same with my knees," the grandfather said. "They've been like this ever since my operation. It must be the scars."

The grandmother came into the room, sat down and picked up her cards.

"There are some advantages I suppose," Stella said. "I don't have to go out and buy a barometer, for instance – I'm a barometer myself. Just listen to it pouring down outside.

Silly of me I know, but whenever it pours like this I always think of Lucien. I'm glad he's got his gravestone at last. At least that'll keep him dry."

Another clap of thunder rattled the window panes. Stella slumped against the side of the table and sat down, her face contorted with pain.

"If I were you," the grandmother said without looking up from her cards, "I'd go and see the doctor."

"It's just old age," Stella protested. "Besides, creaking carts last longest, so they say."

The grandmother looked doubtful.

"I've never known anyone die of good health. You never know what it could be a sign of."

She slapped a two of clubs on the table.

"Small aches great pains, I always say."

CHAPTER 7

THE LAST DAY OF TERM TURNED OUT UNSEASONABLY chilly. Perhaps that was why Miss Veegaete had decided to wear her new dress to school. It looked as if it had been cut from the wings of a rare butterfly. The shade hovered between blue and purple, and lit up in streaks on the skirt and sleeves every time she moved. It was as though the grandmother had taken strips of rainbow and worked them into the fabric.

Miss Veegaete was all dolled up. Her hair was drawn into a flat fold rather like an apple turnover on the back of her head. Framing her face were two locks of hair hanging unfettered from temples to chin in rustic curves. A string of pearls from Thailand gleamed beneath the bolster of flesh at her throat.

The school hummed with bittersweet anticipation. Outside, under the gallery, the breeze rattled the fronds of the potted palms and lifted the yellow crêpe paper skirt around the platform on which the chairs for the notables were lined up.

"Well now boys," said Miss Veegaete, "the Reverend Father will be here any minute to give us his blessing for the holidays."

She stood with her back to the blackboard on which she had written "June: neat and tidy to the end of term" in red chalk. That was four weeks ago, and the letters were smudgy. She had written "time" instead of "term" by mistake, but had quickly rubbed it out.

"What do we say when our visitor arrives?" Miss Veegaete cupped her hands behind her ears demonstratively.

"Good afternoon Reverend Father," the class droned in staggered chorus.

This was not good enough. "Try again! All together now."

After the third attempt she was satisfied. She sat down at her desk, tugged her skirt down over her knees and crossed her arms.

"And now for the animal kingdom," she said, "I wonder what you've brought along to show me."

In fact Miss Veegaete had already shuddered at the sight of some of the boys' contributions. One of them had brought a live hamster, which had been removed cage and all to a windowsill all the way at the back of the room, far away from Miss Veegaete. The rodent pedalled frantically round and round a plastic wheel above the shredded-paper floor of its prison.

Also the stuffed weasel, which was even now waiting on a desk somewhere behind my back, had sent a perceptible shiver of disgust through her limbs. The creature struck a grotesque pose of arrested movement while climbing a branch. It had probably been languishing in some garret for untold years while its rag-wool innards leaked from the gash in its belly.

Another boy had wanted to bring a live stone owl, but the bird had escaped in the night. Miss Veegaete did not seem to mind too much.

Someone else waved a few tatty peacock feathers, possibly stolen from some mother's Sunday hat.

"In nature it's usually the males that go in for display," Miss Veegaete said in her teaching voice. "With humans it's the other way round."

There was also someone who had brought a photograph of a crown pigeon, a very silly-looking bird with an absurd fluffy pom-pom on its head, but Miss Veegaete was enchanted. "Animals in faraway countries are so much prettier than they are here, I always think. In this part of the world it's dreary old raincoats all year round for man and beast alike."

The vibrant blue of her dress made her stand out from her surroundings. Keenly aware that the end was near, I had eyes for none but her. The Day of Judgement was upon us. The sheep would be separated from the goats. We had yet to hear which of us would go home laden with prizes and which would be given homework for the holidays. A few hours from now summer would yawn like a chasm, in the depths of which Master Norbert would be waiting in his grey dustcoat, grinning and reciting multiplication tables.

The bird on the cover of Marcel's letter lay right under Miss Veegaete's nose, on the corner of my desk. One of its wing tips overlapped the postage stamp. I had raised and lowered a corner of the envelope several times with my finger, I had tapped it gently and had even rubbed it with my cuff – in vain I knew – to wipe away the particles of ancient dust that had settled in the creases.

Miss Veegaete ignored me – deliberately, I was sure. From the pheasant she turned to the guinea pig, from the guinea pig to the partridge. I stared at her knees, where a fluttering hand appeared at regular intervals to adjust the hem of her skirt, as if she knew how mesmerised I was by her secrets.

"And what have you got there?" she inquired at long last.

I didn't hear what she said at first, and she had to repeat her question.

I was startled.

"A bird, Miss. The eagle." I picked the envelope up gratefully and laid it in her extended hand.

She gave no sign of surprise. Aside from the faintly knitted brow her expression was blank.

"It's not very clear, I know. It's the postmark. And the envelope's been wet."

"The eagle . . ." she echoed, feigning enthusiasm. She looked straight past me at the class. "When we see a bird with huge claws and a curved beak, what does that tell us? What kind of bird is it?"

"A bird of prey!" shrieked a trio of voices.

"Precisely. A predator . . ."

"It's carrying something in its claws," I said. "See? It looks like an alarm clock with four hands, they look like they're broken . . ."

"I hardly think it's an alarm clock," Miss Veegaete said. "Eagles are rapacious creatures, but they don't fancy alarm clocks. Sometimes they pounce on babies in their cradles.

Not where we live, there aren't any eagles here, but in the mountains there are plenty and everybody knows they snatch babies."

"Perhaps it's a spider, Miss, a fat spider."

Miss Veegaete laid the envelope on her desk.

"It isn't a spider, my boy."

She lowered her eyes, and then, in an oddly quiet voice, she said "It's a swastika."

I had never heard of an animal called swastika. Perhaps they lived in the mountains. Better a swastika than a new-born babe, surely. I was wondering whether I should ask her to tell me more when there was a loud knock on the door. In came the shepherd of souls.

The boys sat up straight. Miss Veegaete drew herself up. She waited for the priest to shut the door behind him and then, just as he swung round to face the classroom, she snapped her fingers.

"Good afternoon Reverend Father," the boys droned.

He motioned with both hands for us to sit down. His cassock stopped just short of his ankles. He wore thick knitted socks and black high-cut shoes with chunky heels, in which he managed to walk without making a sound. He planted his feet firmly one after the other on the green-and-brown speckled floor, zigzagged among the desks, laid a hand on a head here, on a shoulder there, veered round and headed towards the blackboard, where Miss Veegaete awaited him. She dropped a little curtsy, and took his hand in hers.

The priest posted himself in front of my desk.

"Now boys, you must bide your time just a little longer,"

he croaked in a voice that seemed to come from a rusty cogwheel in his throat. "Have patience, the summer holiday is nigh."

He rested one hand on my desk and gestured with the other half behind his back for Miss Veegaete to sit down. She obeyed.

"But during holidays, as at all times," the Reverend Father instructed, "we must all behave . . ." he shuffled his feet, "like good, kind . . ." he took off his skullcap and laid it on my desk, "Christians."

Miss Veegaete nodded in agreement.

The priest moved away from my desk towards the centre of the classroom. "Well, we've got quite a Noah's Ark here, haven't we, with all these animals . . ." he said, and suddenly, as if by magic, his face took on an indulgent, fond look. There had to be a church directory of regulation smiles and benign expressions, I thought, for priests always smiled in exactly the same unctuous way, as if they were posing for a portrait in oils.

"During holidays, too," he went on, "we must do our duty every day. Every day without fail . . . Say the Lord's Prayer . . . some Hail Marys, too. And don't forget to recite a rosary from time to time. And the Acts, of course. Which of you knows the Acts?"

No one moved. The Last Judgement had begun. The shepherd, wolf in sheep's clothing, pillar of black salt, looked round for a likely victim. His large hands, which he held clasped, were level with my eyes. The skin was wrinkled and scattered with tiny capillary veins, the nails were cracked, the fingers bony and tipped with brownish-yellow stains. One of his thumbs rubbed slowly and raspingly over the other.

Looking past him I caught a glimpse of Miss Veegaete hunched over her desk. She had opened Marcel's letter and was reading it attentively, holding her fingers to her forehead.

My heart was pounding in my throat. The priest moved a little to one side, thereby obscuring my view of Miss Veegaete.

Peering from under my eyebrows my gaze left his hands and slid up his chest, past the greasy stains and traces of hastily flicked-off cigar ash up to the wide dingy dog collar and the head emerging from it. The thick, shiny lower lip. The ginger hair protruding from the nostrils. The shaggy eyebrows and bulging eyes which, like his hands, had a tracery of little veins.

The hands separated. One slipped into a side pocket of his cassock and reappeared holding a checked handkerchief. The other hand lay heavily on the top of my head.

"*Allez*, come now my boy, let's hear you recite the Act of Charity . . ."

I braced myself.

"The Act of Charity: my Lord and my God . . ." I murmured, summoning up all my courage to flounder on.

The hand left the top of my head and joined the other hand, and together they raised the handkerchief to the flared, bushy nostrils.

He blew his nose, sounding a fanfare of snot.

I fastened my eyes on the swarm of ink stains and names scratched in the varnish of my desk.

"Normally he is perfectly capable of it," Miss Veegaete gushed from behind the priest's back. "Normally he's up to it all right." The priest turned round. Miss Veegaete hove into view again. She eyed me with dismay. The letter, I could see, was no longer on her desk.

The shepherd was satisfied, now that one member of his flock had been ritually humbled. He strolled down the classroom and pointed to a boy in the back row, who promptly reeled off the whole text.

"Well done. Such diligence is always pleasing to Lord Jesus."

*

The letter had vanished. Miss Veegaete kept her eyes averted from mine, despite my imploring looks. When the priest drew himself up to bestow the blessing she rose from her chair and stared over my head at the class. She crossed herself demonstratively, keeping time with the hallowing gestures of the shepherd as he laved us with the grace of God.

Then it was time for break. I wanted to go up to her, but she hurried off to the coat rack by the door, put on a cardigan (which didn't go very well with the dress, I noticed), and crossed to the priest's side.

There had been a heavy shower, but now the sun had come out again. Everyone was relieved that the ceremony could be held out of doors after all. The village worthies stepped into the courtyard and shook the raindrops off their umbrellas. Miss Veegaete sailed towards them gushing words of welcome and shaking hands. She seemed to swell up all over. Where could she have hidden the letter?

Not on her desk, for it was bare except for the inkwell next to the blotting paper and the tray of pens with crystal handles. In one of her drawers, maybe. The knobs, polished monthly, gleamed invitingly, but I hung back. What if I was caught red-handed?

The platform filled up with bow ties and Sunday hats. The pupils were herded into the rows of wooden benches. The headmaster gave his speech in a voice akin to a wailing siren owing to the faulty microphone, but I was so distracted that I barely noticed. Miss Veegaete was sitting in the front row close to the yellow paper frill, conversing with her neighbour, the priest, who, so the grandmother had confided in me, was not averse to speaking French from time to time.

What had she done with my letter? She must have hidden it about her person, I thought. Slipped it under the elastic of her bloomers, say, in which case it was closer to the secret hairs between her thighs than any human being could conceivably come. Or further up, tucked into the waistband. Perhaps the eagle was hovering over her navel. What if it sought refuge in her bosom, where it would rub against her nipples along with Marcel and his tomatoes as sweet as apples?

There was a burst of applause and everyone turned to stare at me. Only Miss Veegaete went on chattering. Before I knew it I was heading toward the platform together with another boy – he was top of his class, I of mine. We were carrying a heavy basket of fruit between us.

"In gratitude," it said on a card sticking out of the mound of fruit.

Miss Veegaete looked up. For an instant her smile seemed to freeze on her face. Perhaps I was staring at her too fixedly. My cheeks were ablaze. My jaws itched, my tongue groped for something to say, something razor-sharp that would slash her dress to shreds.

The shepherd leaned forward, turned his oily smile on the pair of us, patted us on the head and graciously accepted the basket of fruit.

I was presented with a book about the tundra, entitled *Polar Bears and Volcanoes.* The local photographer turned up to make a group portrait. There was no need to use a flash, as the sun was shining with dazzling brightness – but not brightly enough for me to be able to see through Miss Veegaete's dress.

Afterwards the courtyard was deserted once more. The older boys carried the benches into the school, the potted palms were loaded onto wheelbarrows and taken away.

*

I set off home, and as I went past Miss Veegaete's kitchen window I caught the reek of chips frying in boiling fat, and I could hear meat sizzling in a pan. Louise would be cooking supper. In my mind's eye I saw her patting her wig and glancing furtively at her reflection in the shiny paint on the kitchen cupboards.

No one came to the door – not that I had knocked. Somehow I thought she would appear on the doorstep of her own accord, but there was no sign of life behind the net curtains. Miss Veegaete had made a breach in my soul, a letterbox, envelope-sized.

I turned into the lane leading out of the village, where the asphalt gave way to sand. I looked round one last time, expecting to see her tottering to the corner on her dainty shoes, out of breath and red-faced, waving the envelope. There was no one. The fields sparkled with the lushness of summer. Sparrows swooped down from the poplar trees and flocked round the puddles in the verge. They took flight as I approached, leaving me to churn up the water with my shoes.

CHAPTER 8

FOR DAYS NOTHING MUCH HAPPENED. THE HEAT lay becalmed on the roof, vaporising time. Lulled by the whirr of the sewing machine the hours slid by in an ungraded continuum. The village saint's day was coming round again: for Stella and the grandmother the busiest time of year. Everyone with any status, real or imagined, wanted something smart to wear, even if it was only a new blouse to brighten up last year's skirt, a new collar for a jacket, or at the very least a scarf or a stole, anything for a whiff of sophistication.

The following Monday, when things were more or less back to normal in the house, the church bells rang out in the morning sky. The grandmother had left early to attend the mass for the dead, but more especially to tend the graves of her own dear departed, for she had been too busy to visit them for several days.

Stella woke me up. She hovered around the foot of my bed in her quilted dressing gown and fluffy slippers.

"Come on, get up. I need your help. Now."

The family would be arriving at midday. The corridor was redolent with baking smells. A brace of chickens with knobs of butter on upturned breasts lay ready in a roasting dish on the draining board.

Stella heated some milk and cut two slices of bread. She watched me in silence while I ate my breakfast, bleary-eyed. Seeing my eyelids droop she started chattering.

"There's that Madeira cake I've got to put in the oven. And the soup needs putting through the sieve – you can do that. And you haven't even had a wash yet."

The water in the house was always cold and hard, like a slab of marble shattering into a thousand splinters on my face. I imagined it coming from deep down, from a place never reached by the light of day, hidden in the bowels of the house, gulped down by drainpipes that would gurgle like intestines for hours after a downpour. How much did the water absorb from the dead in the ground before evaporating into thin air, then coming down as rain and sinking back into the earth? The cyclical transformation of water, Miss Veegaete had explained in one of her last lessons, "is a never-ending miracle." I had not seen her since the prize-giving ceremony. On top of the cabinet next to the washbasin stood a glass of water containing the grandfather's grinning false teeth. He was still in bed. The grandmother had her dead all to herself. There were about six that needed grooming.

*

"Hold this while I fix my hairpins."

Stella, seated at her dressing table, had seen me go past in the mirror. The light in her room was tinged puce by the curtains, and the air around her bed was stale from her breath. She inclined her head forwards, guided my fingers to the knot of hair on her crown and opened a box of pins.

"Don't prick my fingers," I said, "I can't stand the sight of blood."

"Can't you do without your fingers?" she laughed. "I thought you didn't need them any more. Not for twisting Miss Veegaete round your little finger, at any rate."

Her eyes gleamed like spotlights.

"Two months from now you'll be in class with Master Norbert, that'll be a different kettle of fish . . . You can let go now."

I laid my hands on the back of her chair. She had put on a close-fitting flowery dress with a low neckline and a zip up the back, which was still half open. Her shoulder blades were dotted with moles, some of which had wiry hairs sticking out.

"Norbert's not as bad as you may think," she said. "At least you always know where you are with him. Calls a spade a spade."

She stretched the hairnet with both hands and fitted it over her bun with a practised gesture. Her fingers knew exactly where the pins had to go.

"By the way," she said, "I've got something for you. You probably left it lying around somewhere. It's in there . . ."

She nodded towards the drawers of her dressing table, in front of her knees. "In the top one. Go on, open it . . . Go on."

The drawers had brass handles shaped like roaring lion's heads with unnaturally long shiny tongues hanging out. I slid the drawer open. At the front, on top of a row of boxes of old face powder, lay Marcel's letter.

Stella fixed me with her eyes in the mirror. I bit my lip and squirmed, wishing I could shrink, turn into a beetle and scuttle away on my six legs to hide in the crack between wall and floor.

"It was lucky for you Andrea was out when Miss Veegaete called . . . Are you going to take that letter out of the drawer or what? It won't bite. It didn't bite you the first time, and it won't bite you now. Go on, take it. I don't want any stolen goods in my room."

"She stole it herself. Stole it from me."

"Keep your voice down. You don't want your grandfather to hear, now do you? Listen . . ." she said, taking both my hands in hers. "I saved your skin, my boy. That's all that matters as far as I'm concerned. You'll have to own up, though. The sooner the better."

"It was only because of the eagle . . ." I protested. My eyes filled with tears.

Stella pulled another drawer open and offered me a handkerchief.

"You might as well cry now. Get it over with. You can tell her it was because of the eagle. She'll understand."

"Can't I just put it back with the others?" I pleaded. "Wouldn't that be all right? I know where she keeps them."

Stella completed her toilette by putting on her round spectacles. The look she gave me was stern but compassionate, like that of a judge in a courtroom.

"You mustn't stick your nose in other people's affairs. To sin once is quite enough. Why don't you thank me with a kiss?"

She drew up her shoulders and pouted her lips. The red on her mouth tasted of raspberries.

*

The afternoon heat rushed in behind the grandmother as she stepped into the hall. She set her handbag on the chest under the mirror and removed her straw hat. Crouching halfway up the attic stairs I watched her kick off her Sunday shoes and crouch in front of the shoe cupboard to fish out her sandals. From the gaping handbag protruded a bottle of bleach, a trowel and the bristles of a wire brush. Over the clasp hung the limp, mud-encrusted fingers of a rubber glove.

I leaped to my feet, screwed up all my courage and called out to her from the unlit stairs: "Grandma, I've got something to tell you."

"Goodness, you scared me out of my wits." she said, startled but in good humour.

I thought I had better do as Stella said and confess right away. I counted up to three under my breath and dashed toward her waving the envelope.

She did not look at me. She did not take the letter.

"Grandma!"

"Not now. Not now!" Her grey curls swung from side to side.

Stunned, I stuffed the letter in my shirt pocket and crept up the stairs to the attic.

Under the rafters the heat was suffocating. Dust danced in the sunbeams pouring in through the skylight and the chinks between the tiles. Outside, the elderberry growing against the south-facing wall was alive with the chatter of magpies. The pigeons scuttled about in the zinc gutter.

I settled down on Marcel's trunk. If only I could just live in the attic. Death was different here. It was sort of friendly, the way it filled the closets, jostling the tangled spectacles, playing carnival with old shirts and meekly retreating when I had had enough.

*

Downstairs was in a hubbub, with Stella going round like a tornado whisking egg whites, kneading dough and chopping vegetables all at once. Plates were set on the dinner table with a loud clatter, the lid of a saucepan clanged to the kitchen floor and a door was flung open.

I heard Stella shout "You can't keep this up forever . . . Damn . . . damn . . ." The door of her room slammed so hard it made the floorboards shake. She was directly beneath me and I could hear her stifled sobs.

After the outburst all went quiet in the house. Geese gibbered drowsily in the orchard.

The grandmother lingered at the bottom of the staircase, her fingers drumming softly on the banister. Then she started climbing, slowly, step by step, pausing to reflect with each step but progressing steadily all the same. I could hear the rustle of her nylon apron. Finally the top of her head rose above the trap door, her forehead, her eyes. She stopped there and raised her arm to beckon me, as if she were drowning, as if she were a creature of the night shrinking from the shaft of sunlight in which I would dismantle her fibre by fibre.

I refused to budge. The attic was mine, it belonged to no one but me. And Marcel.

"Come here, my lamb, come."

I looked down and shook my head.

"You can have the letter. You can keep it. But come downstairs, there's a good boy."

She must have been crying. I had never seen her cry. Her voice was furry with emotion.

"It's not healthy, sitting up here in this oven . . . Come down."

She turned to go downstairs again, but changed her mind. She sat down on a step midway and patted the space beside her. "Come and sit here."

I got up.

She wrapped her arms around her knees. "You mustn't think everyone is as good as they make out," she said.

"And you mustn't be cross with me. I just wanted the bird. Miss told us to bring something to school for the nature class."

"I'm not cross with you. Not with you . . . Not any more."

She stared at her toes peeping out from the straps of her sandals. She pressed her lips together, making her chin pucker.

"She should have given it back to you. You shouldn't have taken it, but nor should she."

Her chin puckered again, her sandals creaked.

"Grandma?"

"Yes . . ."

"I'll look after it . . ."

“I should say so.”

“And when I grow up I’ll go and visit Marcel’s grave. You can come with me if you like.”

She laughed bitterly, sending a ripple across her stomach. “We’ll have to search long and hard.”

“Not if I ask the way.”

“What, you ask the way? In Russian I suppose?”

“I can learn Russian, can’t I? Miss Veegaete says it’s the hardest language of all, but I’ll manage, she says I’m clever enough . . .”

“How would she know? Russian?”

“Miss Veegaete speaks French, doesn’t she? I expect she’s got a gift for languages, she said so herself . . .”

Somewhere between her legs, I thought to myself – between those enormous thighs of hers.

“She’s not perfect, you know,” the grandmother said. “You mustn’t go by appearances, lad. You’re too young, you wouldn’t know. There are things one cannot forget. Forgive – yes, but not forget.”

“The Reverend Father says so too: ‘If you are smitten on one cheek, you shall turn the other cheek’ or something like that, anyway. He’s hard to follow sometimes.”

“He’s not a bad sort, really” she said soothingly. “A bit old-fashioned maybe. But fair. Always has been. A mass is a mass, he said, and it’s not for me to discriminate among the dead. If you skip the flag-waving, then I’ll bury him. Well, it wasn’t a real burial, as there wasn’t a coffin.”

I felt her elbow nudging my hip. She inclined her head toward my ear.

"Your Miss," she said, "didn't dare show her face at the service. Was packing her bags, I shouldn't wonder. Ran off to stay with her cousins in Brussels. Nobody knew her there, nobody had any idea that posh *mam'selle* used to organise German sing-songs and cultural events here in the village. *Kulturabenden*, they called them. A gift for languages, indeed! First she was more German than the Germans, then more French than Louis the Fourteenth. Just goes to show. As for Norbert, he did come to church. He knew it might get him into trouble, but he insisted on coming, seeing as they sent the poor lad for slaughter just like that. He was ashamed of his sister. Embarrassed. She apologised later, when it was all over. Kept writing letters, too, from her boarding school, going on about our Marcel having died a hero and telling me to take comfort in the knowledge that the Lord Jesus sows wild flowers on his grave every spring, for He knows where each and every one of them fell, like so many seeds in the ground. With or without a cross to mark their resting place . . . She's a smooth talker, is our *Mademoiselle Veekàt*."

"Well, she can make her own clothes from now on," I burst out, overconfident now that I knew I would be let off the hook.

The grandmother tapped me on the knee.

"Stand up now, so you can help get me to my feet. And don't you breathe a word to Miss Veegaete, nor to any of my clients. I have a living to make. Off you go. Ask Stella if you can help in the kitchen. My foot has gone to sleep. I'll be down in a minute."

When I reached the bottom of the stairs she called my name.

"About that letter. You keep it to yourself, mind. It's not for anyone else's eyes. Do you hear?"

*

The afternoon capsized over the orchard when the table was cleared and the discussions abated. The grandfather was exhausted from stabbing the air and shaking his fist at the fatherland. He had had too much to drink.

The grandmother bravely went on doing the honours at the head of the table, dispensing sympathetic nods left and right, pats on the arm, and kind words to salve hurt feelings. Now and then a vacant look crossed her face as she twisted her gold necklace round her index finger.

I was at the other end of the table, and Marcel was everywhere. His presence drifted idly on the flotsam of words and kept changing shape in the whorls of cigarette smoke. The grandmother sent me a wink over the array of glasses. Stella, whose nose was still red, gave me a friendly kick against my shins – friendly, but hard enough to hurt.

The uncles and the grandfather downed their *digestifs,* lapsing into silence as they headed towards the parlour. The aunts withdrew to the kitchen. I stole into the hall and grabbed the trowel from the handbag on my way to Marcel's trunk in the attic. Then I came downstairs again and slipped into the sewing room, where I thrust my hand under the fabrics and half-finished garments at the bottom of the wardrobe and pulled out an old biscuit tin. On the lid was a picture of the Queen of Belgium in her wedding dress, smiling vaguely. Her eyes were veiled by a cloud of rust, which struck me as fitting.

*

The day was over-ripe. It bathed the treetops in liquid copper, set the roses ablaze against the west-facing wall and tinged the hydrangeas with a deep blue, like the sea.

I followed the winding paths lined with ground ivy and angelica, past the bed of Cape hyacinths tinkling soundlessly in the wind, all the way to the rowan tree at the bottom of the garden, where my own private wilderness was so overgrown by now that it seemed set upon invading the outermost row of potato plants. I pried the lid off the tin, releasing a faint smell of mouldy almond biscuits. There were crumbs on the bottom. From the kitchen came the muffled clatter of cutlery in the sink. The uncles straggled towards the conservatory at the front of the house.

I took the letter from my breast pocket and unfolded it. "*Molowitz, 28th August 1943,*" it said at the top.

A pair of sparrows flew up from the leafy rowan and perched on a branch of a cherry tree. The geese craned their necks, then thought better of it and subsided into the grass.

Dearest Anna and Cyriel,

Your kind letter has reached me at last. It took more than one month to get here. Russia is a long way away, and the post is not always reliable. This time I received seven letters all at once.

We are quartered in the best building in the village. It's an old school. The people live in cottages with mud walls, not much bigger than kennels. They are very poor. That just goes to show: not all the stories you hear are propaganda, some of them are the bitter truth.

We spend most of the day lazing in the hot sunshine. We also have to guard the workers to make sure they reap the harvest on time. They don't know much about farming. The Ruskies sow their wheat any which way, but the tomatoes are wonderful here. Four, five kilograms per plant, and as sweet as apples.

I'll tell you more about the place later, as I'm short of writing paper. I've got some important news to tell you. They say we will have to take another oath of allegiance shortly. To the Führer himself this time. There's been some grumbling among the men. I don't like the idea myself. Veegaete was against it too at first, but changed his mind double quick when we were summoned by the Hauptmann. "Have you turned Politically Unreliable all of a sudden, Norbert?" he asked. "You've sworn so many oaths of allegiance already, why balk at this one?"

Veegaete hasn't shown his face much lately. Ashamed, probably. Anyway, I've been transferred. I'm with the Grenadiers now, so I'll have a good view of the Russians when the fighting starts. And at least I know what I'm fighting for. For Flanders, not for the Moustache. Politically Unreliable indeed! I hope, Cyriel, that you will soon join us. We need you. Men with ideals are thin on the ground here. There are only three or four who know our glorious Flemish songs. I got up a sing-song a while back, which was a great success.

Thanks, Anna, for the photos, I've put them all up on the wall by my bed. I keep thinking of the good times we used to have in the homeland, and sometimes I have to stop the memories from getting in the way. Thank goodness there are quite a few men from our part of Flanders in our camp. From Lauwe, Bavel, Welle. We're all standing firm.

Give my regards to everyone, especially my sister and Henri.

Not all my letters may arrive, you never can tell. It may be some time before you hear from me again. We've been given marching orders. The Eastern Front beckons.

A hearty handshake and a warm 'Hail' to you all.

Comrade SS Grenadier Marcel Ornelis

*Feldpostnummer 01496*E

I folded the letter again and slipped it into the collar of the shirt I had taken from Marcel's trunk in the attic. I tied the sleeves piously with a rosary given to me by Sister Cécile, which I was glad to be rid of. I stuffed the bundle into the tin and pressed down the lid.

No one had seen me. No one had heard me. Under the trailing vines in the conservatory with its floor of beaten earth the uncles dozed in their wicker chairs. The din in the kitchen had died away. Aunts and nieces would have moved to the parlour by now, putting their legs up unashamedly and nodding off with their buttons half undone to allow for their lunch to settle.

Soon Stella would start cutting the cake and grinding coffee beans, and everyone would wake up. In a moment the entire company would be straggling down the garden paths. The grandfather would sally forth, head high, for all the Colorado beetles had vanished since the day he sprinkled some suspicious looking powder in the watering can.

The uncles had long since lost interest in my little garden, each and every one of them. They would grin, straighten their caps, put their hands in their pockets and turn their backs on my wilderness.

I had no time to lose. I set the biscuit tin at the foot of the rowan tree and seized the trowel. "*In paradisum te deducant angeli.*" I started digging furiously. Rooms aplenty in the earth.

Pushkin Press

Pushkin Press was founded in 1997, and publishes novels, essays, memoirs, children's books—everything from timeless classics to the urgent and contemporary.

Our books represent exciting, high-quality writing from around the world: we publish some of the twentieth century's most widely acclaimed, brilliant authors such as Stefan Zweig, Marcel Aymé, Antal Szerb, Paul Morand and Yasushi Inoue, as well as compelling and award-winning contemporary writers, including Andrés Neuman, Edith Pearlman and Ryu Murakami.

Pushkin Press publishes the world's best stories, to be read and read again. Here are just some of the titles from our long and varied list:

THE SPECTRE OF ALEXANDER WOLF

GAITO GAZDANOV

'A mesmerising work of literature' Antony Beevor

BINOCULAR VISION

EDITH PEARLMAN

'A genius of the short story' Mark Lawson, *Guardian*

TRAVELLER OF THE CENTURY

ANDRÉS NEUMAN

'A beautiful, accomplished novel: as ambitious as it is generous, as moving as it is smart' Juan Gabriel Vásquez, *Guardian*

BEWARE OF PITY

STEFAN ZWEIG

'Zweig's fictional masterpiece' *Guardian*

THE WORLD OF YESTERDAY

STEFAN ZWEIG

'*The World of Yesterday* is one of the greatest memoirs of the twentieth century, as perfect in its evocation of the world Zweig loved, as it is in its portrayal of how that world was destroyed' David Hare

JOURNEY BY MOONLIGHT

ANTAL SZERB

'Just divine… makes you imagine the author has had private access to your own soul' Nicholas Lezard, *Guardian*

BONITA AVENUE

PETER BUWALDA

'One wild ride: a swirling helix of a family saga… a new writer as toe-curling as early Roth, as roomy as Franzen and as caustic as Houellebecq' *Sunday Telegraph*

THE PARROTS

FILIPPO BOLOGNA

'A five-star satire on literary vanity… a wonderful, surprising novel' *Metro*

I WAS JACK MORTIMER

ALEXANDER LERNET-HOLENIA

'Terrific… a truly clever, rather wonderful book that both plays with and defies genre' Eileen Battersby, *Irish Times*

SONG FOR AN APPROACHING STORM

PETER FRÖBERG IDLING

'Beautifully evocative… a must-read novel' *Daily Mail*

THE RABBIT BACK LITERATURE SOCIETY

PASI ILMARI JÄÄSKELÄINEN

'Wonderfully knotty… a very grown-up fantasy masquerading as quirky fable. Unexpected, thrilling and absurd' *Sunday Telegraph*

RED LOVE: THE STORY OF AN EAST GERMAN FAMILY

MAXIM LEO

'Beautiful and supremely touching… an unbearably poignant description of a world that no longer exists' *Sunday Telegraph*

THE BREAK

PIETRO GROSSI

'Small and perfectly formed... reaching its end leaves the reader desirous to start all over again' *Independent*

FROM THE FATHERLAND, WITH LOVE

RYU MURAKAMI

'If Haruki is *The Beatles* of Japanese literature, Ryu is its *Rolling Stones*' David Pilling

BUTTERFLIES IN NOVEMBER

AUÐUR AVA ÓLAFSDÓTTIR

'A funny, moving and occasionally bizarre exploration of life's upheavals and reversals' *Financial Times*

BARCELONA SHADOWS

MARC PASTOR

'As gruesome as it is gripping... the writing is extraordinarily vivid... Highly recommended' *Independent*

THE LAST DAYS

LAURENT SEKSIK

'Mesmerising... Seksik's portrait of Zweig's final months is dignified and tender' *Financial Times*

BY BLOOD

ELLEN ULLMAN

'Delicious and intriguing' *Daily Telegraph*

WHILE THE GODS WERE SLEEPING

ERWIN MORTIER

'A monumental, phenomenal book' *De Morgen*

THE BRETHREN

ROBERT MERLE

'A master of the historical novel' *Guardian*